2005 Contents

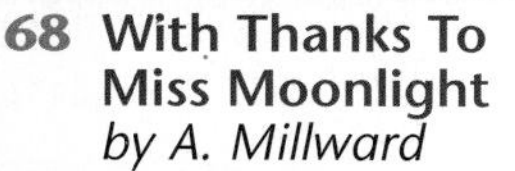

p52

p139

J. Campbell Kerr Paintings

p156

Starting Afresh

by Sally Wragg.

"AREN'T you ready yet?" Chris grumbled amiably.

"Nearly!" Georgia rushed round the flat, seizing bag, coat, shoes, party poppers . . . It was New Year's Eve, and the place was in a mess. There had been no time to do housework. In fact, thanks to Chris, she'd hardly had time to turn round this festive season. It had been one long round of parties and celebrations.

"Will I do?" she asked him at last, taking a deep breath.

"You'll do." He looked at her and grinned. "Just so long as they keep the lighting subdued at this party . . ."

"Watch it, Brannigan." Georgia laughed. She couldn't help herself. But it was good to laugh — it kept her mind off other things.

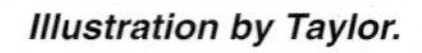

Illustration by Taylor.

"Thanks, Chris," she said, suddenly serious. "I don't know what I'd have done without you this year."

He looked at her and smiled.

"What are flatmates for?" His voice softened. "You deserved better than Andy . . . you always did. I'm only glad I was around to help."

Andy. Georgia could still hardly bear to hear his name. After all, it was only this time last year . . .

She dropped the party poppers into her bag with a frown of determination. Chris had said keeping busy was the way to get through Christmas, and he'd been right.

She had been a complete mess this time last year, though. Hardly surprising, considering the bombshell Andy had dropped last New Year's Eve, only two weeks before their planned wedding.

Glamis Castle

GLAMIS is just over ten miles north of Dundee. In the fertile heart of Strathmore, near the foot of the Grampians, it has everything you could possibly hope for in a castle, except perhaps a moat!

Its outer walls are embellished with sculptures, corbelling, battlements and pepper-pot turrets. To reach the top of the central tower you need to climb 143 steps, and as some of the oldest walls are as much as fifteen feet thick, there's ample space to hide a secret room.

Glamis is the grand baronial seat of the Earls of Strathmore and Kinghorne, and, of course, the present Earl is a cousin of the Queen. The castle's royal connections go back to 1372, but the most famous one has to be Lady Elizabeth Bowes-Lyon, daughter of the 14th Earl, who married Bertie, the Duke of York.

If you've time, don't miss visiting the Folk Museum, now in the care of the National Trust for Scotland. Here, you'll find out all you need to know about farming and working life in this part of the country over the last two centuries.

People's Friend Annua

Dear Reader,

Welcome to the wonderful "Friend" Annual for 2005!

Inside these covers you'll find 30 brand-new stories by all of your "Friend" favourite authors. Whether it's romance, comedy or nostalgia that you like, you'll definitely find something here to suit you!

Follow the characters from our front and back cover in nine charming poems by Kathleen O'Farrell. And it wouldn't be the "Friend", without the beautiful scenic views of Britain by J. Campbell Kerr, would it?

You can also take a toe-tapping step back to yesterday with our series on the Big Band leaders!

You're not going to be able to put it down once you start, so make sure you enjoy every moment that you spend with your special "Friend"!

The Editor

Complete Stories

p94

Poems

p98

Big Bands

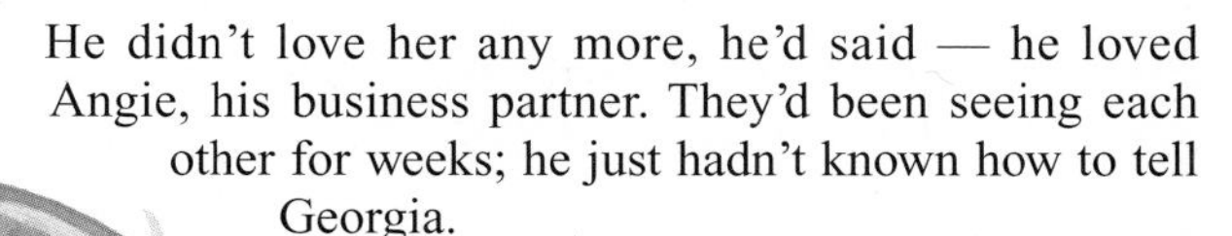

He didn't love her any more, he'd said — he loved Angie, his business partner. They'd been seeing each other for weeks; he just hadn't known how to tell Georgia.

No wonder she hadn't felt like putting decorations up this year; the memories were still raw.

How would she have survived that terrible time without Chris? It had helped, certainly, that Andy had quickly moved both Angie and his business to the other end of the country. It would have been unbearable if she'd been in constant danger of bumping into him every time she'd slipped into town!

"I CAN'T believe a whole year's passed." Georgia sighed now. "But I really thought —"

"What did you think?" Chris prompted softly.

"I thought I was getting over it . . ." Now, she wondered if she ever would. Why, suddenly, did she feel this pain all over again?

"Chris, I'm not sure if I feel up to going out tonight."

He took her hand, squeezing it gently.

"You know what we said," he reminded her. "Keeping busy is the only way to get through this. It'll do you no good, moping around . . ."

She knew Chris was right — he was always right! She nodded her head mechanically, willing herself to accept his advice.

"I'm ready," she said at last. Ready as she would ever be, anyway.

At least, after tonight, the festivities would be over. Perhaps she really could put Andy behind her then, and get on with the rest of her life.

Her hand flew suddenly to her throat.

"I've forgotten my necklace!"

"Oh, good grief!" Chris sighed.

"It's no good moaning — you bought it!"

The necklace had been Chris's Christmas present to her, and she'd fully intended to wear it with this dress. He would just have to wait.

"I won't be a minute!" she cried, rushing into the bedroom and retrieving the gold chain from the dressing-table. She returned, holding it out to him and turning her back.

"Do the honours, would you?"

Chris took an age to fasten the thing for someone normally so deft and precise. She could feel his fingers fumbling against the back of her neck. What on earth could be the matter with him?

Suddenly, those hands crept to her shoulders, and Georgia's heart inexplicably began to thud against her chest.

She turned round and looked up into his face, momentarily lost for words.

He kissed her — only briefly — but it wasn't like the sort of kisses they'd shared before.

"I shouldn't have done that." He stepped back, frowning.

"No, it's OK. I like it, I think . . ." She laughed rather shakily. They were both looking slightly shocked.

"We're going to be late for the party," he whispered.

"It doesn't matter . . ."

And suddenly, it didn't. They both knew something important had just happened.

"What's happening to us, Chris?" she breathed.

Chris was her best friend, for goodness' sake — the first person she'd turned to when her world had fallen apart. Falling in love with him wasn't supposed to happen.

"Chris, I'm nowhere near ready for another commitment yet . . ."

That was putting it mildly. Would she ever be? Georgia sighed. Why hadn't she realised what was happening?

"I can't promise anything . . ." she began.

"There's no rush." He smiled, reaching up to brush a lock of hair from her face. "Let's take our time and just see where this thing leads."

HOW quickly that year had flown, Georgia mused as she made coffee and carried it into the living-room of her little flat. Another New Year's Eve already — how quickly they came round!

She put the mugs down on the table, next to the flowers he'd brought.

"What's up, Brannigan?" she teased. "You're quiet for once!"

Was he sickening for something, perhaps? He certainly looked pale.

"Sorry. It's that obvious, is it?" He made an attempt at a smile and failed miserably. "It's no good trying to fool you," he went on softly.

"There's something I've been meaning to ask you . . ." He took a deep breath. He pulled a little blue box from his pocket, snapping it open to reveal a beautiful sapphire and diamond cluster ring nestling on pale blue silk.

He was looking at her with such longing that Georgia was momentarily lost for words.

"Will you marry me, Georgia?" he whispered.

She took a deep breath, willing herself to stay calm.

Why was she so surprised? Hadn't she half-expected this? Still, it was too much for her — she wasn't ready.

She sat down heavily in the chair opposite him and reached for his hand.

How could she let him down gently? She hated hurting him like this!

"Chris, I'm sorry . . . but I don't think I can."

"I don't understand!"

She could hardly understand it herself, except that she knew, somehow, it would be wrong.

"Because," she began slowly, "I think we've both drifted into this relationship."

It was true. Did they really know what they were doing? Did they even really know each other?

"Georgia, we've been so happy together!" The light had suddenly gone from his eyes. "I know I've been happy, anyway. Surely you've felt the same? I know you have!"

"I have been happy," she admitted.

She had spent a wonderful year with this man, and they'd been growing closer all the time. So how could she put into words what was wrong?

Still, she had to try, for both their sakes.

"When we decided to give things a go . . ." she began slowly, thinking as she spoke. "I wonder if I was really ready — if either of us was?" She stumbled over the words, the sense of it suddenly swamping her.

How could she admit she still thought about Andy, today more than ever. Surely she should have forgotten him by now, if she truly cared for Chris?

IT was raining outside, wet sleet which was usually a portent of snow. Chris dropped the ring back into his pocket and walked over to the window, staring moodily at some party-goers spilling out into the street.

"It's still Andy, isn't it?" he said quietly, guessing her thoughts exactly. How good he was at that! "You still haven't got over him, after all this time." He said it with some degree of amazement.

"It still hurts!" she cried, nettled that he was trying to put a time limit on her healing.

She loved Chris as a dear friend, but it wasn't the same as how she'd felt about Andy, and she couldn't pretend otherwise.

When she had first met Andy, their eyes literally connecting from opposite corners of the room, it had been akin to being blasted by a hurricane! Could she truly say she'd ever felt like that about Chris? They had friendship, a deep sincere friendship . . . but since when had friendship been enough?

"If you're not careful, Georgia, you're going to waste the rest of your life wanting him back." Chris's voice broke into her thoughts. "He isn't worth it — he never was."

"You're wrong!" she cried, despite part of her acknowledging that he was all too right. "In any case, I never promised you anything!"

"No, you never promised anything," he allowed bitterly. "You've been too busy regretting Andy to pay attention to anything we might have!" He swung away from the window. "Must you live in the past, Georgia? Exactly when are you going to start trusting people again?"

She caught her breath.

Did he think she hadn't tried? Betrayal was betrayal — she had thought he'd understood. Georgia felt a sudden spurt of anger.

But then she looked him full in the face. Those eyes looking into hers were full of many things — pain, frustration . . . but mostly love. She tore her gaze away, looking instead at the clock as it ticked the year away.

The room shone. She'd hung garlands of holly and ivy along the length of the mantelpiece, interspersed with red candles and gold and silver baubles.

At least this time round she'd managed to make an effort.

It still wasn't enough.

"I'm not Andy!" Chris moved away from the window to seize hold of her hand with a fervour she hadn't known he possessed. "Georgia, you must know how I feel about you by now! I've given everything to this relationship. What's holding you back?"

He took a deep breath in an obvious effort to control his anger.

"You know where I am if you want me."

He threw her one last, exasperated look and left the flat. She heard him running down the stairs.

IT was barely a minute away from twelve, Georgia realised. A new day, a new year . . . yet she had barely given it a thought. The flowers in their vase on the table had already begun to unfurl — a deep red, almost crimson. How like Chris to bring flowers. Red roses — for love?

How she hated New Year's Eve, and the way it made her think of Andy and his betrayal. No wonder he'd been on her mind! And to think she'd been comparing him to Chris!

The clock began to strike the hour. She could hear shouts and cheers from the street below.

She had let Chris go . . . he must think she didn't care.

She flew downstairs.

Chris was standing under a street lamp, staring hopelessly up at her window. The snow had started to fall, settling on his hair and eyelashes.

"Hello, Brannigan," she whispered, taking his hand.

"Marry me?" His voice was husky.

"I thought you'd never ask." Georgia blinked back tears, more sure now than she'd ever been of anything in her life.

A firework burst above their heads, and the New Year bells began to chime. Chris slipped the ring on her finger and bent his head to hers . . . ■

Illustration by Pamela Goodchild.

The Scent Of Romance

by Joyce Begg.

I NEVER knew why Aunt Fiona came to stay with us to convalesce. Whatever had been wrong with her, she was on the mend. All she needed now was a spell of tender, loving care.

Fiona was my mother's little sister, and though I had met her before, I didn't know her very well. She lived in the city, too far away for regular get-togethers.

My first real memory of her was when my mother and I went to meet her off the train.

Ours was a small country station, tended by Geoff Davis, station-master and frustrated gardener. Each summer, the station platform became a cornucopia of flowers, spilling from an abundance of containers.

Aunt Fiona arrived in winter, when Geoff had ivies and evergreens winding themselves round poles and canopies. Whether sparkling with frost or laden with snow, they were always fresh, and always beautiful.

MY aunt had opened her carriage window and was leaning out as the train came in, anxious to make sure that someone was there to meet her.

"There she is!" my mother cried, setting off along the platform, waving and smiling. "Here we are, Fiona!"

Geoff got there before us, opening the door and taking Aunt Fiona's suitcase. She had started to pull up the window, but he stopped her.

"I'll see to that, miss," he said, with his cheerful, ruddy smile. "They're heavy things, these straps."

"Thank you." She smiled in return. "You're very kind."

"Fiona!" my mother cried, clasping her sister to her tearfully.

Geoff turned to me.

"So you've got a visitor, young Sheena. Aren't you the lucky one?"

"She's my Aunt Fiona," I said confidentially. "She's been poorly, so we're going to look after her."

Geoff looked at my aunt with renewed interest.

"Well, she couldn't be in better hands. If you just give me a minute to see the train off, I'll take the suitcase for you."

Fascinated as I was by our visitor, my attention immediately switched to the train. I never tired of the hiss of the steam, and the distinctive smell that went with it.

The doors slammed, and Geoff checked the carriages and then waved his green flag. The train slowly chugged out of the station.

"Sheena, come and say hello," my mother called. I turned back to meet my aunt.

We made quite a little procession; Geoff leading the way with the suitcase, then my mother and her sister, arm-in-arm, and me bringing up the rear. My mother had arranged for Fred Martin to meet us in his taxi, and we all piled into it.

"That's the case in the boot," Geoff said, sticking his head round the door. "Don't let Fred drive too fast. He thinks he's on a race track!"

Since Fred was known even to me for his lethargy, we all laughed, including Fred himself.

"Thank you again," my aunt said, and Geoff beamed at her. He closed the taxi door, and we set off for home.

The next few days were spent settling Aunt Fiona into the spare room. I was at school during the day, of course, but as soon as I got home, I rushed in to see her. She was up and about most of the day, but from time to time she could get over-tired and had to lie down. The train journey itself had taken a lot out of her, of course.

Dr Spalding came to see her. He was new to our village, having taken over from the old doctor who had been there for years. Dr Spalding was a supporter of the bright, new National Health Service.

I had had one or two encounters with him, the latest being when I had come off my bike and cut my knee. It had required two stitches, which were administered with quiet sympathy on his side and much bravery on mine.

He was a tall man but a bit on the skinny side, I felt.

I preferred Geoff Davis myself — there was something comfortable and cheering about him.

HOW'S your auntie?" my best friend Evelyn asked, after Aunt Fiona had been in residence for ten days.

I looked up from my arithmetic.

"She's all right . . . I think she's getting better. But she's a bit pale." I sighed. "She makes me think of Sleeping Beauty, the way she keeps having to rest."

"Sounds to me as if she needs a Prince Charming — or at least a boyfriend," Evelyn decided robustly.

I was scornful.

"No, she doesn't. She's far too ill to have a boyfriend."

I didn't add that she was also far too old — after all, I was pretty sure Aunt Fiona was nearly thirty! She had obviously missed the boat.

"Stop chattering, girls," Miss Anderson snapped from her desk at the front.

In spite of her youthful dark curls and round pink face, Miss Anderson could be quite stern, and she could certainly get annoyed if you kept chattering when you weren't supposed to!

Evelyn and I returned to our long division — no point in antagonising folk.

* * * *

We went through a spell of truly glacial weather. My mother burned fires in almost every grate, especially the one in Aunt Fiona's bedroom. Even then, the pipes in the house threatened to freeze and ice built up on the insides of the windows overnight.

Getting out of bed each morning was an act of great courage. Washing was perfunctory, and clothes were shot into at speed while you hopped on the icy lino.

"Are you sure you washed properly, Sheena?" my mother asked from her position at the kitchen counter, where she was making my father's corned beef sandwiches.

"Yes," I fibbed, wondering how dirty she thought I could have got since last night's bath. My father winked at me as I started on my porridge.

Aunt Fiona put her head round the kitchen door.

"Good morning, everyone."

"Fiona!" my mother scolded. "What are you doing out of bed at this hour? You'll freeze!"

"No, I won't," her sister said, wrapping her woollen dressing-gown around her. "I was feeling so much better that I thought I'd have breakfast down here for a change. Is that all right?"

"It certainly is." My father smiled, getting up and offering her his chair next to the cooker. "There's fresh toast, and the butter's softening."

The butter warmer was new, and took pride of place on the table beside the bitter marmalade.

My aunt smiled across at me, and for the first time I saw that she was very pretty. Now that the pinched look had gone, I could see that she was fine-boned and delicate . . . beautiful, in fact.

Evelyn's words about a boyfriend came back to me. It would be better if Aunt Fiona were younger, of course, but perhaps there was a chance for her yet. I would put my mind to it.

SHE might like Geoff Davis," I suggested to Evelyn at morning break. "He was very kind to her at the station, and he asks after her sometimes when my dad comes off the train."

"Good idea." Evelyn was slurping the last of her milk through her straw. "So — how do we get them together?"

I had absolutely no idea. If it had been spring, and time for a bit of gardening, I could have imagined Geoff coming along to advise my father on feeding his lawn or planting his early vegetables.

But the grass was rigid with frost and the ground would have broken the strongest spade, so that was a non-starter.

"We could go to the station on the way home," I said. "We could have a chat with Mr Davis — he might suggest something himself."

Evelyn stared.

"You can't just go up to him and ask if he'd like to be your auntie's boyfriend! He'll think you're mad!"

"Of course not," I said hotly. "I'll be more — more —"

The word I was looking for was "subtle", but it eluded me.

In the end, I went to the station on my own, as Evelyn had a piano lesson. She wished me well and demanded to be kept informed.

"Hello, Mr Davis," I said, emerging from the waiting-room on to the platform.

"Well, it's yourself, Sheena," he said, understandably surprised. "You're too early for your dad, pet. In fact, you're in between trains."

Weston-super-Mare

THE long-established resort of Weston-super-Mare is still a firm favourite with families, even in this day and age. It's a very accessible resort, and the prom is flat, as is the pier. Wheelchair-bound visitors can even enjoy the beach, as the flat, compacted sand is so easy to negotiate.

West Tun referred to the tun or farm to the west, and the town was known as plain old Weston until the fourteenth century, when a scribe at Wells Cathedral added "on-sea" (super mare). The town was also one of the first to get a rail link when, in 1841, the first train arrived in the station designed by the master engineer and local boy, Isambard Kingdom Brunel.

If you're looking for sea air that's both relaxing and invigorating at the same time, you won't go far wrong in Weston-super-Mare.

"I know. I actually came to ask you something."

"Oh? How can I help you?" He was on his way up a ladder to snip at some dead ends of greenery, which gave me an inspirational idea.

"I'd like to grow some ivy."

He stared down, as well he might.

"You're interested in ivy?"

I nodded.

"It's about the only thing that grows at this time of year, isn't it?"

"Why, no, not at all." Geoff climbed back down the ladder. "At least, not if you count indoors. Don't you have any hyacinths in your house?"

I frowned.

"I don't think so. What do they look like?"

"You come this way," he said, and led the way through the ticket barrier and across the station yard.

THE station-master's residence was a solid, stone-built house with a large garden. He pushed open the gate and led me past the rows of brussels sprouts and late leeks to the greenhouse at the side of his house.

"There's a couple of hyacinths in here, just ready to pop," he told me. "You choose which one you'd like, and you can take it home."

"But they're yours, Mr Davis," I protested, looking at several little pots with individual hyacinths in them. Most of them were still green, but there was a blue one and a pink one just beginning to scent the air. "Am I too late to grow one myself?"

"Too late this year, I'm afraid. But I can show you how to do it next time. Anyway, I've got far too many." He pointed to one of the little pots. "The pink one's got the best shape. Take that home for your mum, if you like."

"Or my Aunt Fiona?"

His eyebrows rose.

"Or your auntie. How is she?"

"Better," I said. "Shall I tell her you were asking for her?"

"You do that," he said heartily.

So I carried the little plant carefully in front of me all the way home. I worried it wouldn't survive the change in temperature from the warmth of the greenhouse to the arctic air outside, but it was fine.

There was someone coming out of our front door as I approached the house — someone tall and thin, who was laughing as he left. For a moment I was worried, but then I saw it was only Dr Spalding.

He called quite often to check on my aunt, even though she was now so well that she was no longer his patient. It was Aunt Fiona herself who was seeing him out of the door.

"Get back inside before you freeze," he ordered as he headed down the path towards his car. He saw me passing, and greeted me with a smile.

"What's that you've got? A hyacinth? Isn't it perfect!"

"It's for Aunt Fiona, from Mr Davis."

"I'm sure she'll love it — it's a beauty." And he was off.

He was right about the hyacinth. Aunt Fiona did love it, and promised to thank Mr Davis in person as soon as possible.

I was reasonably pleased with that . . . so far so good.

IN fact, that was as good as it got. I tried every device known to man to promote the friendship between Geoff and my aunt, but I got nowhere. They didn't seem to understand the simplest stratagem! In vain, I encouraged Aunt Fiona to call at the station on one of her better mornings. She was plainly puzzled at the very idea.

Likewise, when I asked Geoff what he thought my dad should do with our less than perfect hedge, he came and had a look one Saturday, chatted to my father, and then went straight back home again.

I was very disappointed.

At the same time, there was no doubt that both Geoff and Fiona looked happier. Geoff was always bright and cheerful, but these days there was a new dimension to his happiness.

And my aunt was blooming. Her health was almost back to normal, and there was a glow about her that lit her from within. So my plan seemed to be working.

But they never mentioned each other, and as far as I could see, they seldom met.

Miss Anderson, my teacher, would not have described me as a slow learner, but in this case I was. Even Evelyn got there before me.

"If she's not seeing Mr Davis, she must be seeing someone else."

The penny finally dropped the very next Sunday morning, when Dr Spalding called to take Aunt Fiona out for the day.

I was surprised, because out of the two men, Geoff was much better-looking, at least in my eyes.

But there you go. The doctor was certainly a kind man, and seemed extremely fond of my aunt, which was all that mattered, I suppose.

My mother was ecstatic, and was foolish enough to mention summer weddings and bridesmaids' dresses in my hearing.

Once I got over my astonishment, I was thrilled.

Which just left the mystery of Geoff's inner happiness. I solved that one before Evelyn did.

She had noticed how much less stern Miss Anderson had become in recent weeks, but I was the one who made the connection with the six pots of hyacinths on our classroom window-sill, which filled the air with the heady fragrance of romance. ■

A Proper Little Cupid!

by Sheila Lewis.

Illustration by Ewan McLeod.

MARK followed his mum into the card shop. They were going to buy a birthday card for Grandpa.

"Mum, look at all those cards with hearts on them," he exclaimed. The display of red and pink cards caught his eye immediately.

"Those are Valentine cards," Clare explained. "They're named after St Valentine, the patron saint of people who love one another."

"Are you supposed to send a card to someone you love?" Mark asked.

"That's right. St Valentine's Day is on the fourteenth of this month, the week after Grandpa's birthday. Lots of people will receive cards that day, but they might not know who sent them."

"Why?"

"Because it's part of the fun to make the person guess," Clare told him. "If you send a card, you don't need to sign it — although the person usually knows who it's from anyway."

"Well, they know who loves them," Mark pointed out. "Like you and Dad and me."

"That's right," Clare agreed, and turned her attention to the birthday cards.

Mark lingered in front of the Valentine display, deep in thought. Then he went over to his mum.

"I'll need four cards," he announced.

"Four Valentine cards?" Clare stared at him.

"Yes." Mark was certain. "I need one for you and Dad, and I'll send one to Grandpa, too, 'cause I love him."

"That's a nice idea," she said. "And who else? Maybe somebody in your class at school?"

Mark made a face, even though he knew she was only teasing him. Kirsty, who sat at the same table, was OK, but he certainly didn't love her, so there was no point in sending her a card.

"One for Auntie Bel," he said.

Maybe getting a card would cheer Auntie Bel up. She was always great fun when she took care of him when Mum and Dad went out. The last two times, though, she'd been looking sad, and she kept asking Mum to go into the kitchen so they could chat on their own.

"And another for Hamish," he added.

"Well, good for you, Mark. That's really kind, thinking of everybody." Clare smiled. "You can choose the cards yourself."

He decided that all four should be the same. They had a nice big red heart on the front and a message inside that simply said: *Be My Valentine*.

He wouldn't need to write his name then, so everyone would have to guess who'd sent it.

* * * *

Two weeks later, Andrew Mitchell was surprised to see a large envelope lying on his doormat when he went to pick up the post. And it was pink! A late birthday card? No, that didn't seem likely.

Ignoring the junk mail and the odd bill, he took the mysterious envelope into the kitchen and slit it open with a knife.

Good grief! A Valentine card. At his age! He sat down slowly, a feeling of warmth enveloping him. This was a nice surprise. Someone was thinking of him! *Be My Valentine*. No signature. No other message.

His first thought was that maybe Dorothy had sent the card — her way of saying thank you for walking her dog.

He'd met her when she moved to Willow Close sheltered housing six months ago. He'd often spotted her walking the spaniel, but other than passing the time of day, he'd been too shy to pursue any further conversation.

Then, a few weeks ago, the warden told him that Dorothy had just returned from hospital after a knee operation. The dog had been put in kennels until her owner was fit again.

Andrew called on Dorothy the same afternoon and suggested that he fetched the dog home, offering to walk it every day. He was sure she must be missing her companion, and he could tell that she was touched and grateful for his suggestion.

And so, twice a day, he'd called to collect the dog. On his return, Dorothy always had tea and scones or cake waiting for him.

Sometimes, at the weekend, his grandson Mark had come along, too. Andrew told Dorothy that he'd never regretted moving to Willow Close two years ago after losing his wife, when the old family house got too much for him to look after.

His son, Peter, and daughter-in-law, Clare, Mark's parents, had been delighted. Willow Close was near their house and it meant they could see more of him.

"Mark often pops round after school and at weekends," Andrew told Dorothy. "Sometimes I take him fishing, or rambling in the woods. On wet days we play board games." He sighed. "He's a smart lad. It takes me all my time to keep up with him, never mind trying to win!"

"You're very lucky, Andrew," Dorothy had said. "My family are overseas and I only see them every few months. It's just me and my four-legged friend most of the time."

Andrew looked at the card again. He'd never be sure who'd sent it, but in case it had been Dorothy, he'd do something he'd been planning for a while. He'd ask her to go out with him — just the two of them — for a meal, or a visit to a stately home, or a concert. It was time they got to know each other better.

He looked at the clock. Eight-fifteen. No, it was much too early to telephone her. He'd leave it till around coffee time.

He made himself breakfast and found he was smiling.

* * * *

Bel Heron gulped down a mug of coffee, grabbed her briefcase and unlocked the front door. The postman was on the doorstep.

"Special delivery for you, this morning, Miss Heron." His eyes twinkled.

"You haven't forgotten it's St Valentine's Day?"

Bel managed to thank him, even summoning up a smile.

Stepping back into her hall, she stared at the large pink envelope he'd given her. Her hand was trembling. Surely this couldn't be from Ben — not now?

Only last night, she'd convinced herself she'd finally got over their parting and was, in fact, relieved that he'd taken that job in California. At least there was no chance of bumping into him by accident in town. She'd really loved him and had thought he felt the same about her. However, it transpired that he had plans for his life which didn't include her.

After weeks of agonising and lengthy discussions with her sister, Clare, she'd come to realise that she had to let go.

She opened the envelope and withdrew the card. *Be My Valentine*. There was no signature, no other message.

No, that wasn't Ben's style. He would have put his showy imprint on it somewhere. To her amazement, a wave of relief washed over her. And in that moment, she knew that she was finally over him.

Curious, she inspected the envelope. Few clues there, though. Her name and address had been printed on a computer and the envelope bore a local postmark.

Bel shrugged, then slipped the card into her handbag. It was a nice thought, whoever had sent it.

She stepped out of her house with a light heart and a smile on her face. She had a feeling that this was going to be a good day. Hadn't someone at the office mentioned a Valentine party? Yes, and she'd been too full of misery at the time to accept. Well, she'd soon put that right!

DOROTHY NORMAN heard the letter-box flap open and went out to the hall, followed eagerly by her spaniel. With some surprise she lifted the pink envelope from the mat.

"Good gracious!" she cried. "This is for you, Hamish!" she told him. "Someone has sent you a letter."

She returned to the kitchen and opened the envelope.

"It isn't signed, my pet, but someone wants you for a Valentine," she said to the dog.

Dorothy smiled to herself. Could Andrew Mitchell possibly have sent this? She certainly hadn't pegged him as a romantic, just a charming man with a well-developed sense of compassion. But then, who else knew Hamish better?

No, it didn't seem likely. On the other hand, perhaps this was Andrew's way of saying how much he enjoyed walking Hamish. Yes, that could be it.

There was a certain reticence about Andrew that Dorothy admired, but it seemed to be something of a barrier to a closer friendship. And that was a pity, as she did enjoy his company.

Maybe she needed to make the first move. Why didn't she bake a batch of his favourite scones and deliver them, instead of always waiting for him to call?

She got up from the table and switched on the oven. They'd be ready by coffee time.

PETER found he had little appetite for breakfast. He wasn't looking forward to the morning before him. It had been a mistake to agree to this meeting. Business was good. He didn't need another contract that was going to take up even more precious hours of his time.

Over last night's long, lonely evening in this anonymous hotel, he'd thought about his life and how he had to spend so much time away from home, away from the two people who meant everything to him. Things had to change.

As he was passing reception on the way to the dining-room, the receptionist called out.

"Mail for you, Mr Mitchell." She handed him a large pink envelope.

Peter tore open the envelope. Inside, the printed words read, *Be My Valentine*, but the *My* had a line through it and *Our* was printed above it. There was no message, but he didn't need one. Those three words said everything. He tucked the Valentine carefully in his briefcase.

He had a light breakfast and soon had all the paperwork prepared for his client. He'd explain that his company really couldn't take on the business and give it the attention it deserved, but he had another firm lined up who'd probably suit the client's requirements perfectly.

As an apology he'd give the client lunch and then head home. He might even arrive before the flowers he'd organised!

* * * *

Mark hurried downstairs for breakfast when his mother called him.

"The postie's been," she said and handed him a card.

It was big with flowers on the front and inside there was a message — from Dad. Mark read it aloud.

"I wish I could be with you when this card arrives, because I miss you both every minute I'm away from you — Valentine's Day or not!"

Mark glanced at his mother. She seemed to be wiping a tear from her cheek, but she was smiling, too.

"I hope Daddy got our card. Will he be home tonight?" he asked.

"Oh, yes, I'm sure he'll try to be with us." She sounded happy.

"Can I stay up late to see him?" Mark asked.

"OK, just this once, since it's a special day." Mum laughed.

Mark picked up his spoon to start on his cereal.

"Oh, I nearly forgot. There's another card here. For you," Mum said and handed him a big red envelope.

Mark ripped it open. Inside was a Valentine card. It had a message. *Be My Sweetheart*. There was no name on the card.

He felt his ears go hot. How was he meant to guess who'd sent it? ■

Chestnut Seller

All muffled up, with stovepipe hat,
Hear Charlie Crawford cry,
"Roasted chestnuts —
piping hot!"
To the good
folk passing
by.
"Only tuppence
for a scoop,
So give yourselves
a treat,
For Charlie's chestnuts,
as you know,
Are very hard to beat."

When cold winds blow,
down comes the snow,
And days are drawing in,
He's always there, on
Market Square,
With such a friendly grin.
No wonder he's a welcome sight,
As Christmas time draws near,
With his warmth
and wit — you can
depend on it!
He's part of the
festive cheer.

— Kathleen O'Farrell.

Nan's Day Out

by Donna Watkins.

NAN would take a day trip up to Liverpool every other Thursday during the summer months, and in the school holidays we would go down with Mum to meet her.

It always gave a fillip to my heart to see her step off the train at Lime Street, wave and call "Coo-eee!" when she spotted us waiting at the barrier.

She invariably wore a smart, long jacket and matching skirt, with an incongrous red hat perched on her head. She wore low-heel shoes with a T-bar in patent leather, and fine nylon stockings with a seam down the back.

She would carry a huge handbag, and usually an umbrella. When she bent to hug me she would smell of lavender with the faint hint of mothballs, and sometimes I could feel the little oblong medals of St Anthony and St Christopher that she wore pinned to her vest as she pressed me against her for a quick embrace.

The pattern of the day was set in stone — a trip to Lewis's restaurant for a cup of tea (perhaps an Eccles cake) and a visit to the Ladies' Powder Room (so much more pleasant than the station toilets).

Then Mum and Nan would run the gamut of department stores, my elder sister, Helen, and myself in tow,

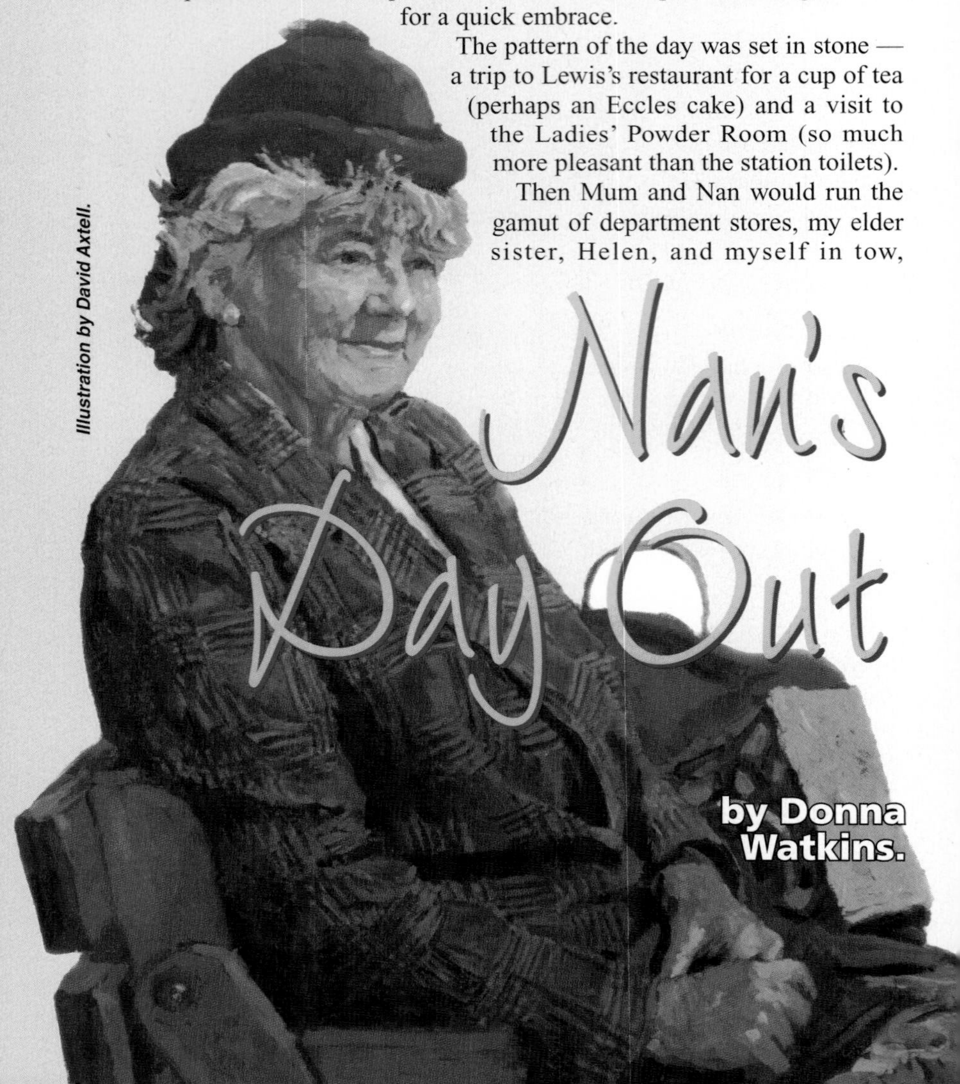

Illustration by David Axtell.

whipping through Ladieswear and Lingerie and Perfumeries until we were giddy.

At some point in the afternoon, Nan would start to flag. Then we'd sit on one of the benches in Church Street to gather our strength. Mum would look strained, sitting on one side of Nan while I sat on the other side, and Helen stood a little distance off, clutching carrier bags.

I would watch the pigeons while Mum and Nan chatted about this and that, mostly Grandad and Dad and uncles and the more disreputable women that currently resided on our housing estate, or in Nan's village.

Then Mum would glance at her watch, anxious to make the most of her chance to shop for clothes and fripperies away from my dad's disapproving glare.

"I'll stay here now, Jane," Nan would say firmly. "You had better go and finish your shopping. I'm all done."

"But, Mum — will you be all right waiting here on your own?"

Nan's face would set in grim determination.

"Of course I will — I'm not a child, you know. If I survived the Blitz in this city, I can survive a few tramps trying to bother me for the price of a cup of tea."

Mum would bite her lip, shrug her shoulders and give in.

"You stay with your nan, Mary. I'll only be another hour or so, then we'll nip into Woolworth's for a cup of tea."

I WOULD nod happily. I looked forward to visiting the Woolworth's coffee shop. I usually had a glass of semi-frozen orange juice from their wonderful orange-juice machine, just visible above the false teak counter, in which whirled three chrome prongs that kept the strands of pulp uniformly mixed among the juice.

Three real oranges floated on top of the juice, bobbing to the tempo of the chrome prongs. They helped confirm the authenticity of the exotic, tangy juice I would sip in ladylike fashion from a heavy-bottomed glass.

"You go on now, Jane," Nan would say, waving Mum away.

Mum would squeeze her hand, then go to join Helen who, as a teenager, was newly converted to the pastime of clothes shopping.

They would hurry away quickly, as though a weight had been lifted from their shoulders — namely Nan and me, too old and too young to keep up with their nimble weaving between clothes racks and boutiques.

When they were gone Nan and I would sit for a while in companionable silence, watching the pigeons as they scurried between people's ankles, intent on scavenging the remains of discarded sandwiches or dropped ice-cream cones.

Then Nan would get her second wind, and turn to me with a conspiratorial air.

Her eyes took on a wicked sparkle and her shoulders would betray a little swagger, like Mae West before she delivered one of her immortal lines.

"Now then, Mary," Nan would say, "what would you like to do? Shall we go and feed the pigeons at the Pier Head?"

"Oh, yes, Nan!" I would always say.

SO Nan would take me by the hand and we'd walk down to the Pier Head, to the square just in front of the Liver Building.

Nan would take out of her handbag half a loaf she'd brought specially, and start to break up the stale white bread into my hand, so I could cast it to the pigeons. Soon, more would arrive and it would seem like feeding the five thousand.

I loved watching them. They had a blue-green iridescent band around their necks that almost glowed against the rest of their dark grey plumage. This was where their feathers had a metallic sheen that altered in the light, and it fascinated me.

There were individual characters that could be spotted in the flock once you had fed them for a while. Some pigeons were timid, some were cocky and comical.

One joker managed to hoop-la a discarded crust around his neck, so that the others were soon chasing him, trying to peck out chunks from his bread necklace.

Nan laughed at this.

"Look, Mary!" She pointed him out. "He looks like a pigeon hippie, doesn't he?"

Sometimes, Nan would encourage me to run towards the mass of feeding pigeons just so I could feel the updraft of their whirring wings as they took off to avoid me, only to return to the breadcrumbs still strewn on the pavement moments later. A Mexican wave of bird-life!

When we had used up all the bread we would look out over the expanse of Mersey (usually a brownish colour even on a sunny day) and watch the *Royal Iris*, the ferry-boat from Birkenhead, dock at the wooden platform.

People would file off, and more people would get on for the return journey. Seagulls wheeled in the ferry's frothy wake as it headed out, and veered back across the river.

Nan sometimes talked about when she was a kid. When she was young she had rickets and spent a while in Alder Hey children's hospital, where she had

Joe Loss was born Joshua Alexander Loss in London in 1909.

He premiered his first band aged twenty-one at the Astoria, Charing Cross Road, and had a big hit in 1939 with "Begin The Beguine".

Never himself a composer, his talent lay in adapting other people's songs. Glenn Miller's "In The Mood" eventually became his theme tune.

After the war his only real hit was "A Tree In The Meadow", but this well-loved, unpretentious man remained a firm favourite.

He died in 1990.

Pictorial Press.

ice-cream for the first time.

Or she talked of when she was courting, about the young men who were her suitors. She would make her prospective dates wait for her at the bottom of her street, underneath the street-light, so that she could check from her bedroom window how smartly they were dressed, and whether they had brought chocolates or flowers.

If they didn't pass muster, she would send one of her little brothers to say she couldn't make it after all.

One of the suitors that did pass muster was Jimmy Delaney.

"Gorgeous, he was," she'd say with a smile and that little swagger. "Just like James Cagney. Oh, I used to love those James Cagney gangster films! Anyway, he wanted to move to America, try his luck in New York, and he wanted me to go with him." Her eyes would grow wistful as she looked out across the Mersey.

"I would have followed him to the ends of the earth, but I was only sixteen. Mum said that I was too young, that I should stay with my family and he could send word to fetch me when he had made a bit of money for himself out there." She sighed.

"I waited years, but no word. Then I met your grandfather and, well, I married him before I heard again from Jimmy Delaney. Too late." She would lean against the rail, musing on what might have been.

"I heard that he made it big out there eventually. Owned property on Long Island, bless his soul."

OTHER times she told me of a boyfriend who bought her a mandolin just because he caught her glancing at it in a shop window on the way to work (her job at that time was rolling cigars in a little factory on the Dock Road).

"Never learned to play it, though." She would chuckle. "But I could dance the Charleston with him real well. Do you know how to dance the Charleston, Mary?"

And she would show me a few steps, and we would end up laughing at our own flapper girl routines as the last few pigeons strutting about us took fright and a few passers-by would stare or smile.

Then Nan would check her watch.

"Quick, we'll just have time to nip into British Home Stores before your mum and Helen try to collect us from the bench," she would declare.

Hand in hand, we would rush past the Victoria monument and into Church Street.

British Home Stores had a hat section on the ground floor back then. This consisted of two mirrors set up at either end of a long, waist-high counter piled with hats which you could select and try on.

Nan loved hats, and so did I. We would start trying them on with systematic abandon, working our way down the counter. Floppy sunhats with false cherries, pillbox hats with filmy veils, Cossack-style hats made with fake fur, or bonnets decorated with dried flowers — we would try them all, mussing up our hair in the process, and laugh or compliment the results.

Then we would hurry back to our bench on the pavement just outside the store, which was next to a concrete tub filled with geraniums and empty crisp packets, and wait for Mum and Helen to arrive.

By the time they joined us Nan would have turned back into the slightly frail, slightly severe, very sensible Nan that Mum expected.

"You two OK?" Mum would ask anxiously, wielding an extra clutch of carrier bags.

"Of course we are, Jane — although I'm ready for that cup of tea before I catch my train back. And I bet Mary wants her glass of orange juice. Thirsty work, sitting in the sunshine, isn't it, Mary?"

And when Mum wasn't looking, Nan would wink at me, her partner in crime. ■

A New Life

by Liz Geraghty.

Illustration by Kiri Hardy.

I'LL be fine, Karys," Margaret reassured her niece for the hundredth time.

"You won't be lonely?" Karys was twenty-six and a dynamic solicitor, but she looked like an anxious infant as she peered up from the driving seat at her beloved Auntie Margaret.

Margaret kissed her, and smiled.

"I'll be fine," she said again. "Off you go now. You've a long drive ahead of you."

"I'll ring tonight," Karys promised. "I'll ring often. And I'll come and see you soon."

"You take care of yourself," Margaret said. "Of both of you!"

Karys's eyes dropped to the soft swell beneath her dress, and she smiled.

"When we arrived on Friday," she confessed, "my first thought was what a wonderful place this will be for my child to spend holidays! It's so peaceful, so beautiful. But I do wish you weren't settling so far away."

Margaret smiled again, but when her niece's car had faded into the distance, she felt a pang of doubt.

Would she really be all right in this new home, a country cottage three miles from the nearest village? It was a hundred miles from Karys, her only living relative, and a hundred and fifty miles from the neat suburban home where she'd spent forty happy years with Michael.

Margaret wasn't one to brood and she busied herself now in the house as she took stock of her new situation.

There was so much to do. Karys had driven her up on Friday. They'd arrived just before the removal van, and they'd spent a hectic hour ensuring everything was unloaded into the right room.

The weekend had rushed past in a flurry of unpacking. They'd barely stopped for meals, chatting as they worked about how the kitchen caught the sun in the mornings; Karys's job; names for her baby.

Between them they'd broken the back of the work. Now, Margaret sorted the odds and ends — the last books found their places on shelves; a painting Karys had hung in the hall was swapped with one she'd put in the sitting-room.

Things were beginning to take shape, but the old, familiar furniture was awkward in its new surroundings. Margaret knew she must be patient. Only time could soften the tables and chairs into belonging. Still, there were a thousand and one little touches she could make to ease things along.

She rearranged her cooking pots and pans until they were orderly and convenient. She hung a favourite photo of herself and Michael where it would keep her company while she ate.

Flowers would be nice, she thought suddenly — she remembered seeing a rich clump of daffodils somewhere in the garden.

IT had been the garden that had caught Michael's eye as they motored past last summer. The midday sun had blazed on the tangle of roses and lupins and sunflowers and geraniums.

"Look, it's for sale," he'd said. And they'd parked the car and strolled hand-in-hand up the garden path.

Margaret took a deep draught of the fresh spring air as she recalled the heady scents of the garden in summer.

The herb bushes lining the twisty path had been in full flower and fragrance — blues and purples of thyme and sage, oregano and lavender.

They'd fallen in love with the place there and then.

Michael had just retired. Although they'd occasionally taken a package tour abroad, their favourite holidays had always been in the English countryside, and this part of the Yorkshire Dales had entranced them.

"Wouldn't it be wonderful if we could live here?" she'd said.

"Well, I think we could," Michael had replied. "We'd love it here."

And — for a while — fate had smiled on their plans.

The estate agent explained that the owners had moved abroad and wanted a speedy sale. Back in Birmingham, they put their own house on the market, and soon closed on an excellent offer. There'd be a tidy sum left over after the cottage was paid for.

And then Michael had fallen ill. Margaret recalled the day the doctor gently told them there'd be no recovery — then she let the memory slide from her. It was still too soon.

* * * *

"Won't you be lonely?" Karys had asked, and Margaret had smiled. Karys was still too young to know that sometimes you have to accept loneliness. Margaret knew that she would miss Michael every minute of every day her whole life through.

And would it be worse here, she wondered, as she deftly snipped the stems of a dozen daffodils? Could she build a new life alone here, where they'd dreamed of building a new life together?

She carried her daffodils back towards the house. The door was almost hidden by an overgrown rambling rose. She could imagine Michael slyly shaking loose petals down on her as they passed in.

"I can't carry you this time, girl," he'd have said, "but here's some confetti."

She left the door open, unwilling to shut any sunlight out of the house.

As she arranged the daffodils in a tall cream vase, Margaret wondered again whether her Birmingham friends had been right.

They'd all advised her to break off the sale of her old house and the purchase of the new. You'll need us, they'd said; you'll need friends around. You'll need a familiar routine to help you through.

Margaret sighed. It wasn't easy. But surely she was right; surely life had to go on, to go forward, not back?

A KNOCK at the door interrupted her musing. She turned, still clutching the vase.

She saw a man standing on the threshold, outlined by sunlight. His height and build were so familiar. She knew a moment's ridiculous delight, as if this was Michael, and then a moment's panic — who could this stranger be?

"Morning. Mrs Whitehead, isn't it? Your groceries are here."

The voice was nothing like Michael's, but the rich Yorkshire accent was so soft and warm that Margaret immediately felt comfortable with her visitor.

"Yes," she said, "I'm Mrs Whitehead — but there must have been a mix-up. I didn't order any groceries, though I had been meaning to sort out deliveries . . ." Her voice tailed off. "Was it Karys? My niece?"

Her visitor laughed and she quickly took in his pleasant, weatherbeaten face and warm eyes. He was a little older than herself, comfortably clad in corduroys and a waxed jacket.

"It was. She called in at Clitheroe's. She said I was to tell you she knows you can manage, she just wants to spoil you a bit. Look, will I bring these in for you? There's a fair load."

Margaret found herself, still clutching the vase of daffodils, leading her first real visitor into her new kitchen.

"Will you have a cup of tea?" she offered. "I'm sorry, I don't know your name."

"I should have introduced myself properly. Tony Robertson." He put down the box of groceries and shook her hand warmly. "I do a bit of driving round the village. I drive a minibus to Kendal once a week; ferry people about in a taxi now and then. Just since I retired."

Tony Robertson accepted the tea gratefully, and he chuckled when Margaret set out a walnut cake she'd made.

"Your niece told me your cakes are famous. She's a lovely girl, and I could tell she thinks the world of you."

Margaret wondered just what Karys had said in the village shop, but she found she didn't mind. Karys had always had an instinct for people. If she'd picked Tony Robertson out as a possible ally, Margaret decided she would trust her judgement.

TONY was easy to talk to, and time flew by as they chatted. She learned that for years he'd driven the post-bus round the outlying farms and villages in this part of the Dales. Five years ago he'd retired, and a month later his wife had died in a road accident.

"I was all over the place for a while," he said. "I don't mind admitting it. We'd always been together. We both grew up in the village, started courting at sixteen and married at twenty. We were wed forty years — then she was gone. I didn't know where to put myself."

She listened to Tony's matter-of-fact voice tell of his bereavement. She didn't want to speak of her own grief — it was too soon for that. But the deep emotion underlying Tony's calm words soothed her spirit. It helped her to think that things would improve.

Only as Margaret saw Tony out through the garden did he make any reference to her loss.

"Your niece told me about it. I think you got a champion lass there, Mrs Whitehead. Nothing'll be easy, but home's where the heart is, and it sounds to me as if you and your Michael planted your hearts right here last summer."

They strolled around. The garden was badly overgrown — spring's rich shoots struggling with dead growth from last year.

"You've a fair bit of dead-heading to do, Mrs Whitehead," Tony said. "And some digging over, and some digging in."

Inversnaid, Loch Lomond

THIS is one of Scotland's best-loved lochs, where life is lived at a tranquil pace amidst glorious scenery. This is where the Highlands and Lowlands meet, and the everyday world seems very far away.

Scottish monarchs as well as monks found sanctuary and peace on Loch Lomond's tranquil islands. Robert the Bruce was given refuge in Lennox Castle on Inchmurrin, and James VI came to hunt the fallow deer.

Loch Lomond has many magical spots, and Balloch Castle Country Park has long been a favourite. Mediaeval knights once rode the ancient lochside paths, and the susceptible Victorians made frequent sightings of the "little people" in the Fairy Glen.

Only a mound remains of the old castle, ancient seat of the Earls of Lennox, and visitors can wander round the roses and rhododendrons of Balloch Castle, the Gothic mansion built by a Glasgow merchant in 1808. Don't forget the delightful visitor centre with rooms of stained-glass panels and delicate murals that create an indoor fairy glen.

J. CAMPBELL KERR.

He surveyed the garden, then looked at her.

"I could maybe lend a hand with the digging. I like to be out and doing in the evening, now spring's here."

At the garden gate they both looked back towards the rose-tangled door. Fresh buds and old flower-heads were fighting for space.

As they watched, a female blackbird chirped and swooped over them, then disappeared into the tangled rose.

"Couldn't be she's got a nest there now, could it?" Tony mused. "Not in with all that dead stuff?"

THAT afternoon Margaret placed her stepladder firmly on the path by the rose bush. She had heavy gauntlets protecting her hands, and a good strong pair of secateurs. She began cutting back the old growth.

It was hard work. She had to put all her power into working the secateurs on the tough old wood, and she had to concentrate hard to keep her face clear of the sharp thorns.

Her hard work paid off. Soon the foot of the stepladder was heaped with cut branches, and the fresh green leaves and pink buds were breaking clear. Something brown caught her eye — surely not a nest?

But it was — a blackbird's nest, spun with age-old skill from paltry scraps. And laid in it, impossibly delicate and perfect, were five pale speckled eggs. It was incredible that new life should be starting there, hidden by dead branches. And yet it was so.

A little worried that her pruning might have scared the mother bird off, Margaret climbed down and cleared away the debris.

After lunch she began work on a border a few yards from the rose bush. She kept an anxious eye on the nest, and after an hour or so her patience was rewarded.

The mother bird appeared. First, she perched on the fence opposite Margaret. Then she hopped further up the fence towards the door. Margaret held her breath, and the bird flapped her wings and glided over to her nest, and settled there.

Margaret felt a warm glow steal right through her. The eggs would hatch and the nestlings would thrive. By the time they were fledged, Karys's baby would be coming into the world, greedy for all the love her mother and her father and her great-aunt would give her.

Perhaps the following summer she'd be toddling on this lawn, being lifted up in careful arms to peep at next year's new eggs in the nest.

There was so much for Margaret to do to make the house and garden ready! She'd be glad of Tony's help, and glad of the friendship he offered.

She'd been right to come here, she thought. And somewhere — always over her shoulder, always just out of reach — she could sense Michael smiling.

"You'll love it here, Margaret, my darling." ■

Danny's Dilemma

by Neilla Martin.

Illustration by Doyle.

IT should have been an idyllic summer. The new house was our dream home — a roomy cottage with a garden full of old-fashioned roses and hollyhocks. It was one of half a dozen set round the green, where villagers often paused to rest on a rustic bench in the shade of a giant sycamore.

There were a few shops, including a post office, and the village school was perfect for Danny. Living there meant that Alan had to drive twice as far to work every day, but he insisted it was worth it.

As I said, that first summer should have been idyllic. And it was — except for Danny.

"I'm bored," he announced as I was pegging out clothes and keeping an eye on the twins, who were sending up scatters of sand from the sandpit.

"You're upside down as well," I said, trying to make him laugh.

He gave up doing a handstand against the cherry tree and glared at me.

"All my friends are at the seaside — and Darren's gone to see his grandma."

"Why don't you play with your little brothers for a bit?"

"'Cause they're just *babies* and I'm nearly *seven*."

He shot me a mutinous look. I could hardly believe this was my normally sunny-natured little boy.

"Darren's grandma makes brilliant cakes," he announced. "Every — single — day. *Fairy* cakes. And she takes Darren swimming and everything."

"C'mon." I ruffled his hair. "I'll make you a banana milk shake — your favourite."

Danny cheered up a bit at that. He finished his milk shake by making loud slurping noises through his straw.

"Why won't my grandma come back from France? She can't make cakes, but she could come here for her holidays just the same."

I thought of my glamorous, scatterbrained mother, trying to renovate a holiday home in the Dordogne and allowing herself to be distracted and delayed by every person and incident she might find interesting.

"She can't come back for a while, Danny, because she's making a lovely little holiday home in France. Maybe we can go there for the holidays next year . . ."

He slid off his chair.

"I'm going to my room now," he said flatly, and left with drooping shoulders and shuffling feet. Tragedy oozed from every pore.

PROPER little sobersides these days, isn't he?" Mrs Budd, the postmistress, glanced at Danny, who was studying the board crammed with postcards which took up most of one wall in the post office.

"That reminds me — I need someone to cut the grass and keep the garden tidy," I said. "Alan just doesn't have time and I only had to cope with a window-box when we lived in town."

"We'll put it on the board beside all the other ads."

Danny followed the proceedings with interest.

"I can read some of these cards," he said with pride, and treated the rest of the customers to a review of the village ads.

The twins started to get restless then, and there were howls of frustration from the double buggy parked by the door. Danny sighed.

"I suppose I'll have to go and get those two sorted out," he said to the queue of customers who were waiting.

There were smiles all round and I breathed a sigh of relief. Danny was getting back to his normal sunny self.

"He's only got one grandma, so he must be missing her," Alan said as we enjoyed a precious hour together when the children were asleep at last.

"And all of his new friends from school are away on holiday, so I suppose he's lonely. Maybe we could stretch the finances to a few days by the sea . . ."

"No, Alan. We agreed about this. All our money's gone on our dream home, so there's no holiday this year. Danny's fine. He's just had to adjust to a new place, new school — and to the fact that his new best friend can't be here all summer," I reassured him.

"And don't worry about the garden. I've put an ad in the post office," I added. I got a hug for that.

I'LL give Mrs Budd Grandma's letter. And it's a *flying* letter, so you've got to give me the money." Danny tugged at my jacket as we passed the post office.

He'd been quiet all morning, playing in his room and ignoring the warm sunshine outside. I was glad that he'd worked up some enthusiasm for posting an airmail letter to the Dordogne.

I chatted to a neighbour while he went into the post office to do his errand. The twins were at their cherubic best for once and revelled in being admired.

"I did it myself!" Danny was back, looking quite cheerful. "What'll we do next, Mum?"

I stifled a sigh. The school holidays seemed to stretch ahead endlessly . . .

* * * *

Mrs Budd stopped at the garden gate on her way home from work.

"I thought I'd better let you have this." She smiled, taking a piece of yellow cardboard from her pocket.

"I found it on the board this morning. Danny must have stuck it there when he was in with his letter."

Grandma Wanted — Danny, it said in vivid red crayoned letters.

I should have been vastly amused, like Mrs Budd, but instead I felt a lump in my throat.

Mrs Budd was beaming all over her plump face.

"A very enterprising young fellow, I'd say." She chuckled. "It's a pity I'm so busy or I'd answer his ad myself."

I could only nod and force a smile. Poor Danny. The dream house was just another house to him. His twin brothers were too young to be playmates and took up most of my attention. And Darren was far away with a grandma who made fairy cakes . . .

"We'll have a baking day tomorrow, Danny," I told him when I went inside.

He managed a wan smile.

"Can we bake fairy cakes?" he asked.

The kitchen was in chaos. The twins were under the table with their building bricks and Danny was standing on a kitchen chair, messily stirring a sponge mixture. There was flour on the floor and footprints in the flour.

As a noisy fight over toys erupted under the table, the doorbell rang.

"I'll get it." Danny jumped off the chair and made for the front door.

"Oh, hello," I heard him say in his clear voice. "Have you come about the job?"

I caught up with him. On the doorstep stood a young woman in dungarees, her blonde hair in bunches, a baseball cap perched on her head.

"She's a bit young for a grandma," Danny said in a stage whisper.

"Can you ride a bike and do you know a lot of games?" he asked seriously.

Our caller laughed.

"Yes to both," she replied, "And I'm pretty nifty with a lawnmower, too."

Realisation dawned.

"You've come about the gardening job," I said.

She nodded.

"I'm Molly. I'm a student and I'm looking for a summer job."

"Come on in," Danny said. "We're baking. You can help if you like."

* * * *

Danny took to Molly right away and followed her around the garden, helping, offering his advice and inspecting all the creepy-crawlies.

Days were spent making Danny's own little garden. Molly hung a sheet from the branches of the cherry tree and she and Danny performed a play for an audience of three, two of whom paid not the slightest bit of attention.

I worried about the amount of time Molly was spending with us.

"Not a problem." She laughed. "Four hours of gardening should keep things ship-shape, and the rest is fun. Besides, I'm training to be a teacher so I need all the experience with children that I can get."

Danny loved Molly's visits and even arranged a baking lesson for her.

"She's not very good, but she's getting better," my son reported one night as I tucked him in. I looked down at a freckled face beaming with contentment.

"You're getting nice and brown," I said.

He nodded happily.

"I bet I'll be browner than Darren!" He giggled.

As I was leaving, a drowsy voice followed me.

"Molly's a great pretend grandma, isn't she? I know she can't bake fairy cakes, but it doesn't really matter.

"And Mum . . ." the drowsy voice continued ". . . I put a card on Mrs Budd's board. Ask her to take it off now, 'cause I don't need it any more."

He hadn't been in the post office for a while. On my way downstairs, I fingered the piece of cardboard in my pocket and smiled to myself. It would have to go into my treasure box. A precious souvenir of childhood . . . ■

Man About The House

by Susie Riggott.

"SHE'S late," Dot said with just a hint of satisfaction.

Letty turned from the window.

The look on her sister's face said it all. Dot didn't want a home help anyway, and this lateness of arrival was precisely what she'd been expecting. She didn't like to be proved right, but . . .

Illustration by L. Antico.

"I expect there's some perfectly good reason," Letty said mildly.

"I expect there is." Dot sniffed. "This is just the start of it, Letty, you mark my words! Turning up at all hours, sloppy work — she'll be more trouble than she's worth."

"Dot, don't start again!" Letty pleaded. Hadn't she heard it all before?

"There's no use making a fuss, dear. This house is simply getting too much for us," she reiterated tiredly. "We've got to accept it — we need help, like it or not."

Besides, she had got her own way in the end. Even Dot had seen the sense in finally accepting that nice Mr Watkins' offer of arranging help with the heavier housework twice a week. But it didn't stop her voicing her objections at every opportunity.

Both ladies suffered from arthritis — Dot silently, Letty volubly. It was just the way they were, like chalk and cheese; the way they always had been, even as children. No-one who didn't know them would ever imagine they were sisters.

Take this home help business, for instance. Letty envisaged some nice young lass and cosy chats over tea and biscuits, and a little life coming into the house for once.

Dot saw loss of independence and too much interference. She'd always been awkward, right from a girl.

At that precise moment, the front doorbell rang.

"There," Letty cried, poised with the teapot in mid-air. "Better late than never!"

"If you say so, dear," Dot replied, a little waspishly.

Ignoring her, Letty hurried to the door to give entry to this nice young lass who was going to relieve her of all the heavier housework, yet still find time for a good old-fashioned gossip. A new friend to get acquainted with! What fun it would be!

She flung open the door. Abruptly, the smile slid from her face.

There was an alien on the doorstep.

That was her first, ridiculous, uncomprehending estimation. She stared at the big, broad body clad in black leathers and a huge black helmet. Letty drew back involuntarily.

"Miss Smedley?" the apparition enquired. Deftly, he removed the motorbike helmet.

"Nigel Brown — I'm your home help. Pleased to meet you. Are you Dot or Letty? Everyone calls me Nige . . ."

He jumped nimbly over the doorstep, splashing rainwater over both Letty and the new hall carpet.

Something seemed to have happened to Letty's voice.

She didn't know whether it was the untidy reddish hair revealed once he pulled off the helmet or the fact that . . .

"But you're a man!" she cried, shock coming to her aid at last.

"Yeah," Nige agreed, grinning from ear to ear. "And a thirsty one. Have you got the kettle on?"

SHE showed him through, hardly daring to look at Dot, though she heard her sharp intake of breath. She went into the kitchen to make fresh tea, listening all the while to the silence in the other room. It was as if Dot hadn't a clue what to say. Struck dumb for once? That was a first, at least.

When Letty came back with the tea, Dot was still rooted to the spot while Nige wandered happily round the room, commenting on photographs and ornaments.

The two ladies watched in silence as he drank his tea and then turned to them with a big grin.

"I'll get started then," Nige said cheerfully. "We'll soon have things ship-shape and Bristol fashion . . ."

Dot's eyes were on stalks when he began to unzip the motorbike leathers, revealing a garish striped T-shirt topped with a grubby white shirt — not even a collar and tie!

Letty frowned. She'd never been one to judge a man by his clothes, but really . . .

"What did I tell you?" Dot hissed, looking affronted.

After accustoming himself to all the cleaning apparatus in the hall cupboard, Nige made a start upstairs. Soon they could hear him singing — something from the "Pirates Of Penzance", wasn't it? Letty was sure she recognised it. She was rather surprised to discover he had a very nice voice.

"Well," she began. "Well . . . at least he's keen."

She had to say something. But what, precisely, had happened to that nice young slip of a thing she'd envisaged? Someone with whom to discuss that Mrs Rogers down the road, or Mrs Bluett, next door, who was expecting a baby, even though she'd five already and where was she going to put another?

Men simply didn't understand that kind of thing, did they?

"I'll ring Mr Watkins," she said, after he'd left. Nige, indeed! Though she really couldn't fault his work.

He'd been through the house from top to bottom, constantly refuelled, it seemed, on the tea Letty had spent the rest of the morning making. She'd never known a man drink so much tea.

"I'll be back on Friday." He'd grinned, climbing back into his leather biking gear, apparently having no idea of the consternation he'd caused. "Mind you don't make too much mess in the meantime, ladies . . ."

They heard his motorbike roaring off into the distance. Letty got straight on the phone.

"Can I help?" Dave Watkins' voice was infinitely reassuring.

Letty proceeded to fill him in on all the morning's traumas.

"We just weren't expecting a man . . ." she finished lamely.

"Perhaps I should have warned you . . ."

If Letty hadn't known Dave Watkins better, she might have thought he was smothering laughter.

"Are you dissatisfied with his work?"

"It's not that . . ."

It wasn't, either. Nige's work couldn't be faulted. The house was positively gleaming, Letty thought miserably, looking round. He'd even dusted the aspidistra by the phone on the hall table.

Letty noticed, because she'd meant to dust it herself earlier.

But how could she explain about the chats she'd so been looking forward to? That a man simply wouldn't do?

"I'll come and see you," Dave Watkins said patiently.

What a nice man he was. And Letty did accept that, in their right places, men could be very useful.

"Perhaps I'll reorganise the rota," he said, "and find you someone else, if it's really what you want. Only I'm afraid I'm rather busy at the moment, so it won't be until next week at least."

And that appeared to be that. Miserably, Letty put the phone down. It didn't sound as if anything might be sorted by Friday, Nige's next scheduled visit.

The two old ladies awaited the day in some measure of trepidation . . .

* * * *

"Morning, girls!" Nige called cheerfully, dumping his biking gear over the back of the dining-room chair. "Have you missed me?

Big Bands

Duke Ellington

Born in 1899 in Washington, DC, Edward Kennedy Ellington grew up to lead one of the definitive jazz bands of the 1930s and 40s. He acquired the nickname "Duke", apparently, because of his wit and intelligence.

Duke Ellington left his home town to go to New York, and was soon playing at the famous Cotton Club.

He wrote a whole number of great swing classics as well as more serious pieces. His theme tune in the early days was "East St Louis Toodle-oo", and later "Take The 'A' Train".

Duke Ellington died in New York in 1974.

Pictorial Press.

Dot's face went a bit mottled, as if she were holding something in, very tightly.

"I'll put the kettle on," Letty broke in tactfully and hurried off into the kitchen.

She made tea. Nige stood in front of the fire, smiling happily, perfectly at home. He still looked untidy and dishevelled, but he smiled conspiratorially at Letty.

"WHO'S the lady next door?" he asked, a gleam of real interest in his eye.

"Mrs Bluett?"

"*She's* going to have her hands full," he observed, taking the tea.

"I counted five little 'uns this morning, and another on the way by the looks of it. Where's she . . ."

"Going to put them all?" Letty actually laughed out loud. Fancy that thought crossing Nige's mind, too. She leaned forward.

"Do you know," she said, "I've wondered the very same thing myself!"

"Are you two going to stand there gossiping all morning?" Dot asked, feeling suddenly left out.

"Letty, this man's got work to do."

"You're right enough, ducks," Nige agreed pleasantly. "And when I've finished this tea, that's just what I'm about to do!"

He set to. The ladies could only stand back and admire — the place had never looked so clean.

"Hiya, gorgeous!" he called, passing Dot on the stairs.

Dot gazed stonily ahead and went on up to her room to collect a library book. Gorgeous? Had she heard him right?

Suddenly, a little hiccup of laughter escaped her. It was a long time since anyone had called her that.

And dashed, Dot thought, laughing all over again, if she didn't rather like it.

"I'd have got that for you," Nige said, concerned, when she came back downstairs, book in hand. "You'd only to say."

"Right, Nige," Dot agreed. "I will do next time!"

"Will there be a next time, do you think?" Letty asked, wondering about Dave Watkins and the telephone conversation.

The two ladies sat having lunch. Nige had gone about half an hour earlier. The house seemed strangely quiet.

And was it any wonder, without this strange man bustling about the place, the constant whistling and singing, the stopping to have a little gossip when he thought Dot was otherwise occupied?

It hadn't taken him long to work out Letty was the one who enjoyed a good gossip. It seemed Nige liked nothing better either.

AT that moment, they heard the doorbell ring. Could it be Nige back again? Maybe he had forgotten something? Eagerly Letty rushed to the door, smiling happily.

"Morning, Miss Smedley." Dave Watkins stood on the doorstep.

"I'm a bit earlier than expected. And I have good news." He beamed, laying his bulging briefcase on the front room table.

"I've managed to jiggle things around. If Nige does a swap with Rachel Hewins, who looks after Mr Carsington in Wimpole Street, and someone takes over her afternoon session at the old folk's home . . ."

"What?" the ladies interjected simultaneously. "Who?"

"Rachel Hewins," Dave explained. "A young girl. I thought you'd be pleased . . ."

"The very idea . . ." Letty said, scandalised. "Some young slip of a girl who probably wouldn't even know a Mrs Bluett from — from a blue *bottle*!"

"But — if you aren't happy having Nigel as your home help . . ."

"Whatever gave you the idea?" Dot cried, not to be outdone. "Absolute nonsense, young man!"

No-one to call her gorgeous? She smiled happily at the recollection. Nige's next visit wasn't far away.

Dave Watkins looked from one to the other, bemused.

"But I thought . . ."

"We're very well suited, just as we are, thank you," Dot said stiffly. "Our Nigel's quite good enough for us."

* * * *

"It's funny, isn't it?" Letty commented later, as the sisters sat in the spotless kitchen, enjoying a fresh cup of tea.

"What's that, dear?" Dot asked absently.

Her sister laughed deliciously.

"Why, us, silly — having a man about the house at last!" ■

The Grandmother

Beside the market stall she stands,
A book of verses in her hands,
So engrossed, that Charlie's cry
Of "Roasted chestnuts —
come and buy!"
Falls upon deaf ears,
it seems,
For Grandmama is lost
in dreams . . .

These poems such
memories evoke
Of yesteryear, and
those dear folk
Who, though they've gone
beyond her ken,
She still loves now as
much as then,
That Grandmama will
not demur,
Surely this book was
meant for her!

And so, in hours of
quiet content,
When, by her fire,
alone sits she,
In friendly lamplight, this small book
Will be such pleasant company,
A book to treasure, thoughts to share,
Bought for a song, on Market Square!

— Kathleen O'Farrell.

IT was early morning, very early in the morning, in fact. The sun had still to show its face. Richard plodded carefully up the steep incline, half feeling the way with his right hand, brushing the tips of bushes and long grass to help negotiate his way and keep his bearings.

He was thankful his trainers kept a good grip on the worn, sandy path. Today would be a bad day to have a mishap.

Every so often, he'd look down at the large and cumbersome object he carried in his left hand, as if to make sure that it was still there.

Underneath his green padded jacket he wore a jumper, soon to be changed to a shirt and tie, with, of course, the new suit.

But all that would come later. For now he needed warmth, for it was a cold, dull morning.

Pausing at the summit, he wiped his forehead with the back of his hand. He could feel the pitter-patter of his heartbeat, and the rasping of breath in his chest, and he stopped and stretched to ease the slight stitch in his side.

He was a short, thickset man, who looked younger than his sixty-two years. The breeze flattened his recently trimmed hair, causing the greyness at his temples to stand out starkly against the rest of the mahogany brown.

He blew his cheeks out, staring down at the scene below. It always calmed and reassured him to see the waves far below, their continual motion that never ceased.

Letting Go

by Veronica P. Norman.

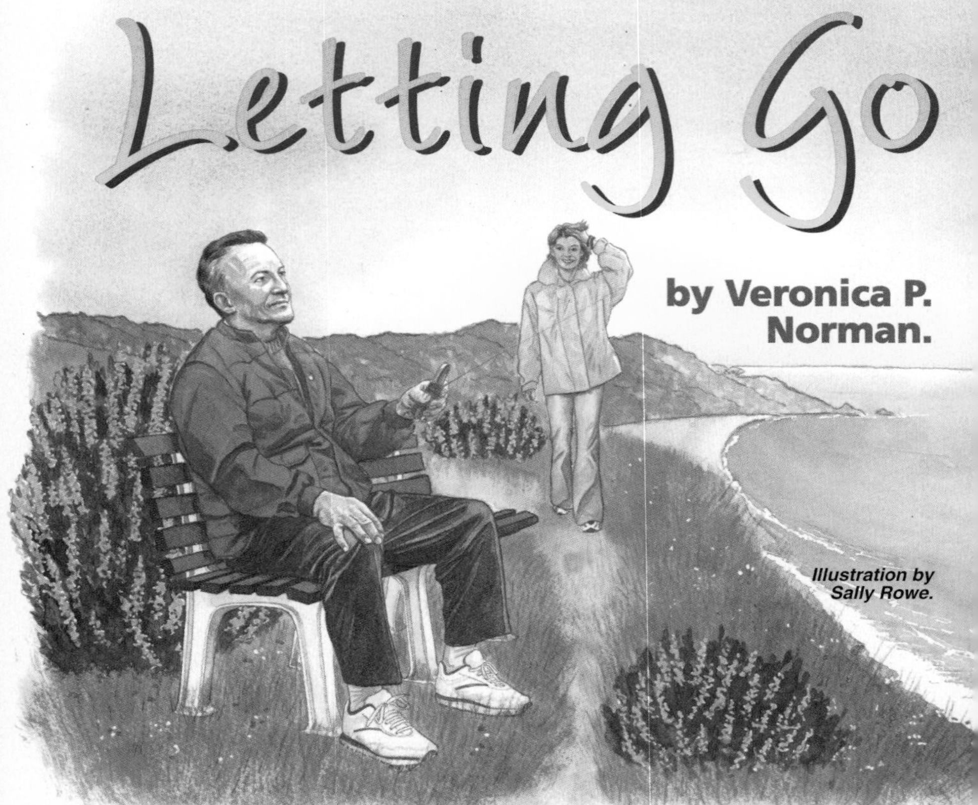

Illustration by Sally Rowe.

Today he felt he needed something reassuring, something usual — heaven knew what the rest of the day would be like.

WALKING over to the now-weathered bench, he sat and carefully set down the burden he'd been carrying. It was a red kite.

He unwound the white tail and studied the kite. It was still fine, as fine as the day he'd made it, twenty-five years ago.

Twenty-five years! That was how old his daughter was.

He remembered sitting at the kitchen table as soon as he'd got home from the hospital, his heart full and so excited that he couldn't possibly go to sleep.

He'd made several phone calls, had gone and told their neighbours the news, but still couldn't settle.

He'd had an urge to stand by the gate and inform every passer-by that at last, he and Davina were parents to a beautiful little baby girl!

Josephine — the name they'd chosen months before, after his grandmother and Davina's sister. It would have been Philip if the baby had been a boy, but Josephine had always been his favourite.

Richard unwound a length of string from the spool, and glanced up towards the horizon. The sun was beginning to rise and the breeze felt cool against his forehead.

Looking down at the beach, he caught sight of a couple of joggers setting forth from the far side of town. They looked as small as ants. Idly, he wondered whether they were tourists.

He played out sufficient string and walked a few paces from the bench to set the kite flying. As if in encouragement, the breeze started to gust a little and he quickly launched the kite up into the clouds.

He sat back on the bench and thought again of that time, that special time, twenty-five years ago, when he'd first flown the kite.

After assembling it on the kitchen table, he couldn't wait to see how it would fly. Grabbing hold of it, he'd almost run all the way — he'd been a lot fitter in his late thirties — though he'd also stopped to tell everyone he saw the incredible news.

Up here on the cliff-top, with the waves breaking far below him, the distinctive smell of the seaweed and the salty breeze on his face, he'd thrown the kite up into the wind and watched it rise.

Seeing it soar high into the sky and almost disappear into the clouds, he'd felt such great elation and joy! He'd felt that he could do anything, that he could conquer the world — that it was all his for the taking, to give to his new baby daughter.

Watching the kite now, a tiny dot in the sky, he smiled at his memories. Life had been simple then, with no conflicting emotions, and after flying the kite, this same kite, repaired and mended several times over since then, he'd suddenly succumbed to his exhaustion and gone back home to bed.

Nine hours solid he'd slept, until the braying noise of the alarm clock woke him just in time to go and visit his brand-new family at the hospital.

When she was still but a babe in arms, he and Davina had brought Josephine up here to watch the kite fly.

She would stare, fascinated, her chubby cheeks made scarlet by the wind and her big brown eyes large with wonder.

Watching her captivated by it, Richard had felt his heart fill and overflow with affection for her laughter, her innocence and her youth.

When she was eighteen months old, he'd given her the string to hold. She thought she was flying it all by herself, and grasped it tightly with her chubby little fingers, unaware of Davina's hand close by.

She had chuckled her own peculiar infectious chuckle, pulled and jerked the string with determination written all over her face.

He'd looked across her head and met Davina's eyes, smiling back at him, and he'd known then that he was completely happy, and so lucky to have them both.

He never forgot the moment; it was pressed like a flower, deep in the memories in his mind.

PULLING at the string, he stared up at the dancing kite. The sun was now well over the horizon and caught the tail in its strengthening rays, turning the white to silver and flashing a welcome to the morning.

Richard sighed. How quickly the years had flown.

He and Josephine had come up here throughout her childhood. There had been different kites, lots of them: stunt kites, box kites, a kite that whistled and kites in the shape of eagles and dragons. They'd flown them all.

Sometimes, Davina had watched, sitting on a tartan rug on the grass, picnic by her side; sometimes, a couple of Josephine's school friends had joined them. And sometimes, the best times of all, it was just Josephine and him together.

How they'd talked on those occasions, discussing their favourite colours, their favourite meals, whether they'd sit on the new bench when the council eventually put it up. Later, it was about the sort of job she wanted, problems with teachers at school, and how to put the world to rights.

Richard wondered whether Josephine ever remembered their conversations, and how she'd once said, "I'll never leave you, Daddy. I'm going to stay with you and Mummy for ever and ever and ever. You're the only man in the world for me."

He could see her face, earnest and quite serious, her deep brown eyes looking right into his. He remembered the way her arms had snaked around his neck, and how she'd hugged him, hard, before jumping up suddenly, snatching up the blanket and yelling, "Race you home, slow coach!"

And away she'd scrambled, laughing her head off, down the cliff path like a small puppy stealing a slipper.

His eyes were wet with unshed tears, and he loosened the string almost to its fullest length from the spool, causing the kite to fly higher, fluttering and straining in the strengthening wind.

There wasn't much time left now, and he sighed as he surveyed the area below. There were several more people on the beach below — dog walkers, solitary joggers, even a family of four, walking along the shoreline.

"Enjoy them while you can," he murmured. "They'll be gone before you know it."

AS if in answer to his words, he suddenly heard her voice.

"Dad, what are you doing up here?"

There was a flash of movement and there she was — his Josephine. Dressed in her bright yellow jacket, with blue jeans and trainers, she flung herself down on the bench beside him.

"Thought I'd find you here," she said, pushing her fingers through her windswept hair. "What on earth are you doing, Dad? There's no time to be kite flying now.

"Mum's going frantic. Aunt Hilda's flapping around like a mosquito and —" She broke off and stared at him.

"Are you OK, Dad?" Her voice was suddenly gentle, and she placed her hand questioningly on his sleeve.

"What's up, Dad? Aren't you feeling well? You're not ill, are you? Oh, Dad!"

Her voice ended in a slight wail, and Richard turned sharply towards her, as if only just aware that she was there.

"Hush," he soothed, feeling her need for reassurance. "It's OK, I'm OK. I just wanted a bit of peace and quiet, before it all gets going. Before . . . before it all starts."

"Yes," she agreed, snuggling into his shoulder, "it has all got a bit manic, hasn't it?" She giggled, her usual childlike giggle. "Auntie Hilda came downstairs as I set out. She still had her curlers in and was looking like a porcupine!"

Richard smiled at her description and put his arm around her. She leaned her head against his shoulder.

"Dad?" she asked.

He glanced across at her.

"It won't be the end of us, will it, you and me? You know, coming up here and flying kites?"

"Of course not," he replied, making his voice as hearty as possible, trying, without realising, to dispel his own fears as well as hers. "Though whether Tom will mind you disappearing up here for hours at a time is a different matter. You can come up here with me whenever you like — though it may not be so easy when the babies come along." He smiled.

"They'll just have to come up here, too, like you and Mum brought me! How old was I, four months?"

"Younger, I think," he replied. "Can't really remember."

"Well," she said calmly, "we'll bring them up and fly with them." She glanced up at him, her eyes mischievous. "You can carry them up!"

Staring into her face, he felt ashamed of his previous thoughts of loss and despair, and he hugged her briefly before releasing her.

Did all parents feel like this on the day their children married? Had his parents felt this way when he'd married Davina?

Of course, there wasn't all the fuss and confusion beforehand like there had been in their house for the past eight months. But still . . .

He wondered whether he'd have felt differently if they'd had more family, whether other children would have diluted his love for her. No, he decided, he wouldn't.

She started speaking again, gazing into the horizon, squinting into the sun.

"I'll still come here, Dad, I'll still come up here with you and sit on this bench. I may be all grown up now, but I'll always be your daughter."

She gazed at him with an unwavering stare, and he realised that she was right. Nothing had really changed except that life was going the way it was meant to.

All he really wanted was her happiness, and he knew she would be happy with Tom, who looked at her in much the same way as he looked at Davina.

"You're right, sweetheart." He hugged her. "I'm sorry if I worried you. It's just all the fuss and palaver. Today will be great, and I'll be the proudest man alive, walking you down the aisle.

"Anyway, we'd best be going or all our planning will go awry. I'll just sort this out —" he nodded up to the kite, hardly visible now in the sky "— and then I'll come home.

"You go on ahead and put the kettle on. We'll have a quick cuppa before I take you to the hairdresser's. Can't have you looking like Aunt Hilda, can we?"

"OK, Dad." She kissed him briefly on the cheek. "I'll be waiting."

She laughed gaily as she started back down the path, a lightness in her step that hadn't been there before.

HE followed her retreating back until she was gone before starting to wind in the kite. It was pulling now, dancing with the high winds up above, so high that Richard fancied it was probably touching the undersides of the clouds.

He stared up at it, squinting into the morning sun.

Suddenly, he started unwinding it from the spool, feeling its strong pull as the kite soared even higher and higher. Smiling, he realised that he'd reached the end of the string, and he held it for a second with finger and thumb, its end nestling in his palm.

Then, with a sigh of reconciliation, he released it, watching it circle once as if in farewell and then fly higher.

"You have to let go some time," he murmured as it became first a speck in the sky, and then vanished completely from his sight. ■

Kirriemuir, Angus

A STATUE of Peter Pan takes pride of place in the centre of Kirriemuir these days. This is because Kirrie is the birthplace of J.M. Barrie, the man whose pen created the original boy who never grew up.

Anyone driving through its narrow streets and wynds will instantly see why this is called "the little red toun", as nearly all the buildings are of a distinctive dark red sandstone.

Kirrie is built on the sunny slopes of the Braes of Angus, on the left bank of the Gairie Burn. The burn once powered looms for the thriving linen industry, though in spring at the Den, it's hard to credit the industrial past of such a peaceful place.

Remember to visit the cricket pavilion at the top of Kirriemuir Hill. The pavilion's unique — it's also a camera obscura, one of only three in Scotland. You can enjoy a sweeping panoroma over Strathmore, and away to the heathery mountains beyond the Angus Glens.

THE fair came to our town every year. Salthaven was on the coast, and though smaller than most of the great resorts, we had our faithful visitors. Some said that the population of the town doubled over the summer.

I wasn't so sure about that, but it was certainly worth the fair's time to stop in Salthaven for a week, and we looked forward to it with uncontained excitement.

There were all the usual rides — the chair-o-planes, the waltzer, the dodgems — as well as the shooting range, the coconut shy, and enough candy floss for sixpence to make you sick.

"I'm going on everything," my best friend, Marion, declared.

"I'm going on everything except the ghost train," I said.

"Coward," was Marion's reply, but she was smiling.

"Just commonsense. Look what happened to Agnes Tully."

Our teacher had once told us that Marie Antoinette's hair had gone white overnight with terror, which was understandable, given what eventually happened to her. According to Salthaven legend, Agnes Tully's hair had done the same thing in the three minutes it took to ride the ghost train.

Unfortunately, there was no way of verifying this with Agnes herself, since she had

Fairground Attraction!

by Elizabeth Harvey.

left Salthaven for foreign parts some time ago, but the legend lived on.

"It hasn't happened to anyone else," Marion said reasonably.

"But you never know," I said. I was either more imaginative than Marion, or more gullible. I suspect the latter.

Anyway, the ghost train sounded petrifying. Even Billy Watt said it was scary, and though Billy might not have been the brightest button in the box, he didn't lack courage. If he said it was scary, that was enough for me.

MY sister Rose came with us to the fair. Rose was eighteen, and I was nine. Normally she would have chosen more mature company, but she came along, ostensibly to keep an eye on us.

In fact, she did nothing of the sort. Rose had other fish to fry. His name was Joe and he was in charge of the dodgems. She had met him on the Monday, the first night of the fair, and had been irresistibly drawn back.

"Do you think he's her boyfriend?" Marion asked.

I shrugged.

"Don't know."

"He looks really nice."

"How much money have you got?" I asked, more concerned about how far our finances would take us than anything Rose might have in mind.

It was half an hour later that we got round to the dodgems.

"My turn to drive," Marion yelled as we piled into a bright blue car.

We watched as Joe swung his way round the cars, taking the money. Marion smiled up at him cheekily, but I looked straight ahead. Rose was standing on the rim, waiting for him to come back to turn on the power.

After that, it took all our concentration to avoid being shunted, particularly by Billy Watt. I didn't look for Rose again, intent as I was on screaming directions to Marion.

"SO how was the fair?" my father asked when we got home. He looked over the top of his newspaper from his seat at the fireside.

The fire wasn't lit, and the evening sun was lighting up the table by the window, but he sat in his usual chair just the same.

Illustration by Heidi Spindler.

"OK, I suppose," Rose said, looking out of the window with a secret smile.

"And how about you, Sheila?" He shook his paper. "Did you have a good time?"

"Great," I said. "You should come, Dad. You'd really like the hall of mirrors. Everyone likes that. And you could get your fortune told."

"Ah. Well, that might be interesting. I wouldn't mind crossing the ocean or finding my fortune. Did you go on the ghost train?"

I shook my head. When I looked him in the eye, I could see he was smiling at me, though he didn't say anything. I didn't like to explain about Marie Antoinette. It sounded daft in our living-room. And anyway, I knew that was only an excuse.

"Well, you've got a few days left," was all he said. "Plenty of time."

"I'm not going to go on it, Dad. It might be dangerous."

He laughed.

"What is life if you don't take a few risks?"

Rose turned from the window with an odd look in her eye, but before she could say anything, my mother came into the room and the subject changed.

NEXT night, Marion and I gave the dodgems a miss and concentrated on winning a prize at one of the stalls. I was really after a goldfish, but got a penny whistle instead. I was less than enchanted. However, at least I could shove it in my pocket when we went on the chair-o-planes.

The wonderful thing about the chair-o-planes was the view. I could see why people wanted to be pilots when I was up there. I wouldn't say I could see the whole town, but I thought I caught a glimpse of our house on my third revolution, and of course I could see everything that was going on in the fair itself.

It was Marion who spotted Rose and Joe. They were standing very close together at the ice-cream stand.

I craned my neck to keep them in view, and on the next circuit I saw them wandering between the stalls, laughing and nudging each other. At one point he put his arm round her shoulders, and then I lost sight of them again.

I also saw people emerging from the ghost train, and though no-one was actually white-haired, there were some pretty terrified-looking people. What I didn't quite grasp was that one or two of those who looked the palest were rushing to queue up for another go.

There was no doubt that the ghost train did exert a strange fascination. Even matter-of-fact Marion felt it.

"Come on, Sheila. We've got enough money. I really want to go on it."

"Maybe tomorrow. Let's go on the waltzer."

And like the good friend she was, Marion gave in.

That night, I went home on my own, once my path had separated from Marion's.

Rose was still out, and my mother tutted at her for leaving us to our own devices. She *was* supposed to be looking out for us.

My father asked me again if I had gone on the ghost train, and I had to confess that I hadn't.

"What I think," he said, "is that half of you really wants to do it, and the other half is scared. The thing is, Sheila, that you've got to face your fears in this life."

"Leave the girl alone," my mother said, plumping cushions before she finally sat down. "It's only a ghost train."

My father smiled at me.

"That's perfectly true, of course. But I think you'll regret it if you don't do it. *Courage, mon brave*." The last bit was French, but I knew what it meant just the same.

I had been in bed some time when I heard Rose come in. She opened my door on her way to her own room, and whispered my name.

"Sheila? Are you awake?"

"Yes," I murmured, still thinking about the marvellous sensation of the chair-o-planes.

"Did you go on the ghost train?"

"No. Marion wants to, but I'm still scared of it. Have you been on it?"

I could see her shaking her head in the light from the hallway.

"But I'm thinking about it."

"Dad says that half of me wants to do it, and the other half is scared, and the only way to deal with that is to be brave. He says I'll be sorry if I don't."

Rose was surprised.

"It's only a ghost train."

"He says life is like that."

There was a small silence.

"Well, maybe you'll work up your courage by Saturday."

"Maybe."

"Goodnight, Sheila."

"Night," I said sleepily.

SATURDAY was the last day of the fair, and Marion and I had worked out exactly how we were going to maximise our time and money. We passed Billy Watt firing in every direction on the shooting range, but that held no magic for us. It was to be the dodgems, the hall of mirrors, and I was still considering the ghost train.

My parents came to the fair that night as well. I was quite surprised to see them, my father in his sports jacket and tie, as always, and my mother in a cotton dress with flowers on it and a nipped-in waist. They strolled around arm in arm, which I found both endearing and slightly embarrassing.

"Where's Rose?" my father asked. "We haven't seen her at all."

I shrugged, but something stopped me from mentioning Joe. I diverted them by suggesting that we all go to the hall of mirrors.

It was great to see my mother laughing like that. She was a bit serious normally, my mother. They were still laughing as they wandered off towards the hoopla, and Marion and I made for the candy floss stall, our finances secretly boosted by my father.

We passed the dodgems while still enmeshed in candy floss, but there was no sign of either Joe or Rose. It was an older man who was swinging round collecting the money. Joe must be on his break again, though Saturday was their busiest night.

It was when Marion threatened to ask Billy Watt if he would go on the ghost train with her that I realised the moment had come.

"I'll go. I can do it."

She dragged me to the queue before I changed my mind.

Billy Watt was right. It was scary. As the carriage trundled through the flap into the darkness beyond, the noises started.

Wails and groans and clanking chains assaulted our ears. Luminous skeletons dropped in front of us, and white-sheeted ghosts came straight for us with gaping mouths. Bones rattled, and cobwebs draped themselves across our hair.

I was absolutely petrified, and could imagine weeks of nightmares as a result. I have never been so glad to see daylight, even dim evening daylight, in my entire life.

There was not one particle of pleasure in the experience, and nothing would induce me to go again. But I had done it.

AS a special treat, because it was the last night of the fair, we were allowed up late, so that it was dark by the time we made for home. Marion's parents had appeared later on, and it became quite social. Even Rose materialised out of the gloom, and walked alongside Marion and me. Although I sensed her mind was on other things, she wasn't unfriendly.

"So did you go on the ghost train in the end?" she asked.

"Yes," I said casually.

My father had said he was proud of me, but no matter how nonchalant I tried to sound, I was still shaking with fright.

"Did you go on it, Rose?"

"No," she said quietly.

"So you didn't take the risk?"

There was a long pause before she spoke. Her voice was regretful, yet filled with an unexplained relief.

"I thought about it, Sheila. I thought about it long and hard — but, in the end, I chickened out. There'll be another ghost train, some other time," she said. "Life's like that sometimes, I suppose. But, I'm not sorry. I'm not sorry at all."

I was confused by what my sister said, but she just smiled at me, and for the first time in ages, she took my arm and walked with me, like we used to. ■

The Perfect Dress

by Liz Gilbey.

MY feet are killing me, Gran! Can I have a cup of tea?"

Stacey Green collapsed on to the settee in her grandmother's sitting-room, scattering bags and parcels around her.

At four o'clock on a Saturday afternoon, after a day-long bout of serious shopping, she felt there could be nothing more welcome than a hot, restorative cup of tea!

Rita Bowden clicked the kettle on, and gave her granddaughter a sympathetic grin.

It was, she recalled faintly, the most difficult thing in the world to be nineteen and on a major mission to impress.

"Any luck today, then?" she enquired mildly.

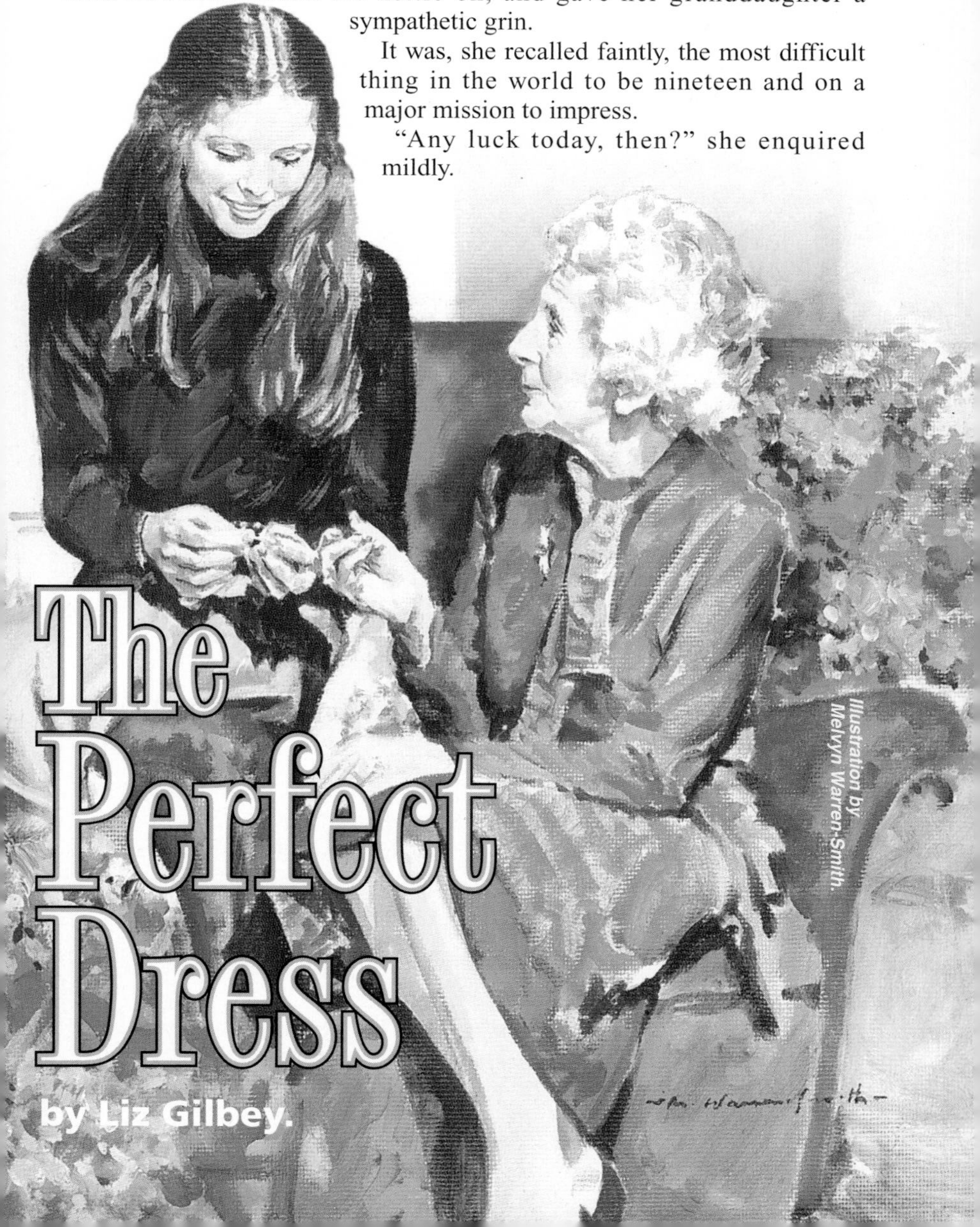

Illustration by Melvyn Warren-Smith.

"Well . . ." Stacey pulled a face, then rummaged around in a large, expensive-looking pale turquoise carrier bag and drew out something black. "Yes — I bought this. It's just I'm not very sure about it now I've got it out of the shop . . ."

Rita stepped forward to take the garment from her youngest granddaughter. It was a simple wisp of a black dress, elegant, sophisticated, expensive, classic. It was gorgeous.

Rita glanced at Stacey, puzzled.

"It's beautiful. What's wrong with it?"

Stacey made a face.

"I think it might be a bit too old for me. I'm worried that it might turn me into lamb dressed as mutton!"

They laughed together, and Rita resisted the temptation to agree.

THE trouble was that Stacey had an important dinner-dance to attend the following weekend — her first really grown-up, dressed-up event. Her new boyfriend, Graham, had invited her to go with him to the annual party his computer firm gave for top staff and rising stars. He had seemed flattered suddenly to be classed among this elite.

And when he'd asked Stacey to accompany him, even though they had been going out together for just seven weeks, she accepted graciously — and only panicked about having nothing suitable to wear after he had gone home!

"What do you think, Gran?"

Stacey wrinkled her nose in the way she always did when something was troubling her.

She had always been the one closest to her grandmother, and the two shared tea, gossip, confidences and a great deal of laughter on Stacey's visits to Rita's little bungalow.

"I think it's a lovely dress. Why don't you go into my bedroom and slip it on so you can show me properly? And while you're doing that, I'll make us that cup of tea."

Stacey went off obediently, clutching the little black dress. But as Rita was pouring the boiling water into the pot, she heard Stacey's call.

"What are you doing in here, Gran? The place looks like a bomb has hit it!"

Rita poked her head round her bedroom door. Wardrobes and drawers were flung open, and the duvet upon the bed had disappeared beneath a pile of clothes.

"No-one's tidied up for me while I've been out of the room then?" she grumbled jokingly. "What a shame!

"Shirley next door is organising a jumble sale on Wednesday, and I agreed to give her some things. The trouble is, I ran out of enthusiasm for sorting all this stuff about half an hour ago . . ."

"Don't worry, Gran, I'll help you. We'll soon get it done!"

Stacey modelled the black dress while the tea was poured. She twirled around the kitchen, a fine mixture of enthusiasm and doubt, and Rita thought she looked trim, pretty and eyecatching — but not really like her Stacey at all.

The dark colour and classic, simple lines were beautiful, but they aged and sobered her bright and charismatic granddaughter.

"You look very nice, you really do. Elegant," Rita began, trying to be positive.

"I know!" Stacey exclaimed. "But it's really not me, is it?"

Rita hesitated.

"Well — perhaps in five or ten years' time . . ."

"I knew it, I knew it!" Stacey threw herself down on a chair in frustration. "I want my dress to be perfect. This dinner-dance is so important to Graham!"

"You really like him, don't you?" Rita asked, and watched as Stacey flushed a gentle shade of pink.

"Yes, Gran, I really do. I know I'm still only nineteen, and we haven't been going out together for very long, but it just seems — right, somehow. It's like we've always known each other. We're not out to impress or anything silly like that."

"That's just how it was with me and your grandad. We just knew, almost from the minute we met. Together for ever."

SHE handed Stacey her mug of hot sweet tea, and they drank in companionable silence across the kitchen table.

Yes, she and Roy had always been together, from teenagers until the end, Rita reflected. Forty-six years together, and not a single day regretted. That was something to be proud of.

She hoped Stacey would be as happy in her life and relationships as she had been. She had only met Graham once, so far, but Rita had instinctively liked the sturdy young man with close-cropped brown hair and quiet dark eyes.

Stacey drained her cup.

"It's a lovely dress, but it won't do, so I'd better return it. Back to square one — I still don't have anything to wear. And I'm running out of time!"

She looked so glum that Rita had to laugh.

"All this trouble about you finding a dress — and I'm getting rid of a load of mine!"

Stacey grinned at her grandmother. Her eyes fell upon a photograph in a black leather frame that had hung on the kitchen wall for years — a holiday snapshot of a young couple who laughed directly into the lens of the camera. They were on a beach with their arms around each other — a young man with wavy red hair and a contagious smile, a young woman with twinkling eyes and a striking resemblance to Stacey herself. They could almost have been sisters.

Stacey had always loved that photograph. It gave off a feeling of sunshine, fresh air and the simple joy of being alive and together.

It was such a good likeness of her grandparents, too.

Perhaps that was why it had always been kept in a favoured spot on the kitchen wall — not in splendid isolation amid the formal grandeur of the sitting-room, but by the kitchen window, in the heart of the house, where all the important business of daily living was done.

Rita followed her granddaughter's glance, and found herself gazing at the photograph, too.

"You've always liked that photo, haven't you? So have I. Whenever I look at it I'm taken back to a wonderful day . . ." She smiled to herself.

"I love your frock in that photo, too!" Stacey said unexpectedly. "I always have!"

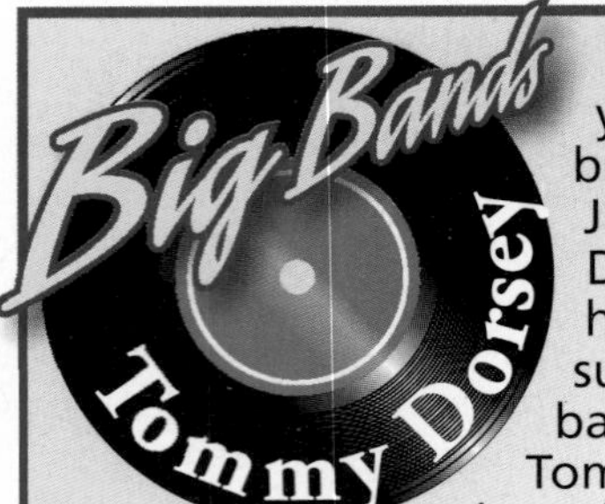

The younger brother of Jimmy Dorsey, himself a successful bandleader, Tommy was born in 1905 in Shenandoah, Pennsylvania.

Along with his brother, he formed the Dorsey Brothers Orchestra in 1930, featuring artists like Glenn Miller, Ray McKinley and Bob Crosby.

A disagreement between the brothers in 1935 saw Tommy leaving to form his own band.

The tune, "Sentimental", became his theme, though his biggest-selling record was "Boogie-Woogie".

Although he also played trumpet, it's as a trombonist that he is remembered as one of the world's most successful recording artists.

Tommy Dorsey died as a result of an accident in 1956.

Rita laughed, taken by surprise.

"Have you? You've never said before. I've always loved it, too. I suppose that's why I kept it safe all these years."

Stacey gasped.

"You've still got it?"

"Oh, yes! It has so many special memories for me, I've never been able to bring myself to throw it out."

TOGETHER they went back into Rita's bedroom to brave the piles of clothes spread out on the bed and floor.

Rita went straight to her largest wardrobe, and without hesitation reached into the back, and from under a protective cotton cover pulled out a patterned blue dress.

It was in a silky, sky-blue material, very mid-Fifties in style. The blouse-like

Pictorial Press.

top had a fitted bodice, tiny capped sleeves, a stand-up collar, starched high lapels and a V neck. The tiny waist, with side zip, led down to a full and flounced skirt.

IT was the sort of dress, Stacey thought, that film stars of the Fifties always wore. The styling was classic, but it was the material itself that made the dress so special.

Around the hem, tall stems of golden corn, white bindweed, darker blue cornflowers and poppies cascaded up the skirt in a riot of colour.

"It looks just like a summer's day," Stacey said, transfixed.

She remembered the first time she'd really looked at the dress in the photograph.

She was only a little girl, but she knew the dress was special — just seeing it had made her feel happy, even then.

Two weeks later, Rita put the summer's day dress back into the wardrobe where it had spent so many years. She smiled to herself as she did so.

Perhaps it was because granddaughter and grandmother were so alike in looks and shape at nineteen that the blue dress fitted Stacey as if it had been specially made for her — and it suited her fair skin and auburn hair just as it had suited Rita's all those years before.

Of course, it had been inevitable that Stacey would try on the dress, and neither she nor Rita had been surprised when it fitted perfectly and looked so beautiful.

And both of them, without saying a word, knew exactly what Stacey would be wearing to that important dinner-dance.

With her hair caught into a high ponytail and decorated with a tiny corsage of garden flowers, elegant court shoes and a tiny clutch bag, which Rita had found wrapped in tissue paper at the back of the wardrobe, Stacey had gone to the dinner-dance looking young, beautiful, self-possessed, fresh and charming.

Looking, in fact, very much like herself.

She had been a bit worried as to whether or not Graham would like the dress, but he seemed to be bowled over by her unconventional attire, Stacey had gleefully reported back to her grandmother.

He was never one to gush, but his simple "You look absolutely gorgeous" had been completely heartfelt and sincere.

STACEY was quiet for a moment as she remembered her wonderful night. Rita looked at the faraway expression on her face and suddenly remembered Roy's eyes when he had first seen her in the very same dress. She nodded and smiled contentedly.

Stacey took a deep breath and continued with her story.

"Even Graham's boss complimented me on the dress! Everyone else had played safe with little black dresses — or dark blue ones.

"He said I looked like a breath of fresh air and as welcome as summer sunshine on a dark day. I think Mr Grayson is a bit of a charmer!"

"Or you are!" Rita teased.

"Do you think I might borrow the dress again some time? I think it's lucky."

Stacey looked up, concerned, as her grandmother did not reply at once. Rita's face was uncertain.

"Borrow it again? But all the dinner-dance people will have seen it once already, and it's so distinctive . . ."

"Oh, no, not for anything like that."

Stacey shuffled her feet, almost embarrassed, but always happy to share a secret with her grandmother.

"I think I might be needing it for an engagement party some time soon." She grinned, somewhat sheepishly, as her grandmother's hands flew to her face in delight.

"But keep it quiet for now, will you, Gran? We haven't mentioned anything to Mum and Dad yet."

Rita Bowden swept her youngest granddaughter into a hug and laughed out loud.

"Well, that puts rather a different slant on things!" She wiped a tear from her eye.

"I think we can bring that old frock out of retirement once more for such a special event! Especially as your grandad proposed to me when I was wearing that dress!" She looked down into Stacey's bright eyes, twinkling with tears of happiness.

"But I warn you, I don't have any wedding dresses hidden away. Nor any little black dresses, for that matter!"

"So who needs a little black dress?" Stacey said, with an airy wave of her hand. "Not me! I'm much happier without one!" ■

A Lifetime Of Love

by Alison Lewis.

Illustration by Sala.

"THE car will be here in a few minutes, Mum. If you're sure you're ready, I'll go, then, and meet you at the church."

My daughter, Janet, bustles into the room, organised and efficient as usual.

"Let's look at you. Have you got everything?" She looks at me closely. "Oh Mum! If you cry your make-up will run. Here . . ."

Janet fusses around me with powder and powder brush, like an anxious make-up artist on a Hollywood film set. I stand quietly and let her, because underneath her brisk, businesslike exterior, I know she is feeling at least as emotional as I am. Janet has never been given to showing her feelings, even as a little girl.

"There, that's better." She puts the powder away in her handbag and then, firmly but gently, takes the photograph from me and puts it back on the table, next to the lamp where it belongs.

"Right, Bill," she says to her brother. "I'll be off. Make sure you keep her calm. I'll see you in a few minutes, Mum."

She disappears, and the room is strangely quiet. Bill looks at me and smiles but, understanding, says nothing.

My eyes stray back to the photograph I had been gazing at. It's a small black and white print, taken on my wedding day in 1943.

George and I both look very young in it, but so happy; perhaps the fear over what the future might hold made us even more determined to enjoy our special day.

We had known each other all our lives. Our parents lived next door to each other, and George was two when I was born.

We were friends and playmates from the time that I could toddle. When we were eight and six respectively, we solemnly told our parents that we were going to get married when we were older.

Twelve years later, we said it again. I didn't honestly expect my parents to agree — after all, George was only twenty, I was eighteen, and he was about to go overseas to war.

Perhaps because they knew our hearts were set on it, or perhaps because we knew each other so well, they agreed after all. I still remember how happy we were when we heard their decision.

THE wedding was arranged quickly as there was very little time before George had to leave to go to the war. I wore my best blue dress. It was chilly for June, and Auntie Elsie, who we all thought was "posh", lent me a short fur jacket.

Our garden had been dug up for vegetables, of course, but my mother had saved a couple of precious rose bushes, and they provided enough pink flowers to make me a small posy.

Mum and George's mum pooled their rations, and we managed to have a small wedding cake and a wedding breakfast for a few friends and relations at our house.

We couldn't afford a honeymoon, even if we'd had time, but Auntie Elsie and Uncle Albert went to stay with Mum and Dad, and let us have their big house for a couple of days.

We always said that we would have a proper honeymoon one day. Somehow we never did get around to it — there was always something else taking priotity.

Now, waiting to go to church, I look at Bill. He is the image of George — tall, dark thick curly hair, and brilliant blue eyes.

George always had a warm smile he kept especially for me. Bill's smile is loving, but no smile could ever be like George's.

"The car's here, Mum. Are you ready?"

I smile, suddenly nervous. Bill passes me my bouquet — pink roses again, but there the similarity to that first posy ends. This one is pink roses, with creamy white freesias and ferns.

I check my appearance in the mirror — lavender dress and jacket, and the kind of hat I have always dreamed of wearing, large brimmed and decorated with tulle and roses, with a small eye veil. I find myself wishing that George could be here to see me now, shy and excited as a young girl; but, of course, he isn't.

I gasp with amazement when I see the car.

Janet and Bill arranged it, and I knew they were planning a surprise. A black, gleaming Rolls Royce is parked outside my house, white ribbons fluttering on the bonnet, the back window decorated with pink and cream flowers.

As Bill hands me into the car, I feel like royalty and I can't help thinking of that first wedding again. Then, Dad and I walked to the church, and all along the road women popped out of their front doors to see me go, and to wish me well.

WHEN we reach the church, the vicar is there to greet me, with Janet and my granddaughter Sarah, who is my bridesmaid, waiting to make sure I'm tidy.

"Phyllis, you look wonderful," the vicar says, kissing my cheek. I've known him for years — he officiated when Janet married and he christened Sarah. He winks at me. "Everything's fine — he's here!"

Janet comes forward to straighten my dress, and her eyes are suspiciously misty.

"Oh, Mum." She puts her arms around me and hugs me. "I do love you."

She hurries into the church, embarrassed by this unusual display of emotion. I know she loves me, but Janet has never been given to expressing it in words.

I look at Sarah, standing elegant and beautiful in the background. She has been watching me silently and unsmiling since I arrived. I wonder whether she thinks that I'm a silly old fool, that romance and dreams are just for the young.

Suddenly, her face breaks into a radiant smile.

"You look marvellous, Granny," she says, "and it's all so romantic!"

The photographer fusses around taking a few photographs, and then slowly we move towards the church door. The vicar gives the organist a sign, and the building fills with the sound of magnificent organ music.

"All right, Mum?" Bill smiles at me. "You really deserve this, and I'm absolutely thrilled for you." He squeezes my arm.

"Here we go then!"

As we walk slowly up the aisle, I am conscious of the sun streaming through the stained-glass windows, casting dancing coloured patterns on the congregation, and the flowers on the ends of the pews, arranged by my friends from the church.

The church is packed with friends and relatives, but suddenly I only have eyes for my groom, standing at the front of the church.

His hair is silver now, but still thick and curly.

As he turns to look at me, his eyes are as brilliant a blue as ever, and he smiles that warm, loving smile that he has had for me for as long as I can remember.

George has always been a romantic, and it was his idea that to celebrate our diamond anniversary, we should renew our vows and have the wedding we could not have the first time around.

He and our children made all the arrangements and now, after all these years, we are finally going to have the proper romantic honeymoon we always promised ourselves in Paris.

We smile at each other as I reach the altar steps, and then turn to listen to what the vicar is saying.

"I would like to welcome everybody to the Church of St Barnabas on this special day, to witness the renewal of George and Phyllis's wedding vows, and to celebrate with them a lifetime of love and companionship."

A lifetime of love. I could never wish for anything more. ■

YOU won't be able to miss Ashbourne, sitting in its lovely valley on the edge of the Peak District, if you allow yourself to be steered by the tall steeple of St Oswald's Church.

For such a small town, Ashbourne has a church of cathedral proportions. Charles I, newly defeated at Naseby, attended a service at St Oswald's in 1645 and it truly is a magnificent building, well worth visiting.

During the Napoleonic Wars three hundred French prisoners were held at Ashbourne. They earned their keep and had quite a bit of freedom — some even went on to marry local girls.

One Frenchman, working at the bakery, persuaded the baker to try a little ginger in his biscuits — and so the world-famous Ashbourne gingerbread was born!

J. CAMPBELL KERR.

With Thanks To

HARRY JOHNSTONE was really going to miss this place. He was surprised by the strength of the feeling himself, but there were others who would be absolutely amazed by it.

School — noisy dinner halls and squeaky floors, too cold in winter, too hot in summer.

It was funny how he looked at all these things so differently now that the time had come to leave them behind for ever.

The tiny, red-curtained, draughty hall in which they'd had their final assembly earlier had almost seemed cosy today.

by A. Millward.

The piano they sang along to in music lessons hadn't sounded half as out of tune as usual, and even the teachers didn't seem that bad.

It was typical, wasn't it? That the day he realised he quite liked being here was his last day, too. The day when a big part of his life came to an end and another was just beginning.

FOR a long time at Redbricks Primary School, Harry had been an "under-retriever". At least he thought that was what the headmistress used to say. Personally, Harry liked dogs, so he didn't see what was wrong with that, but he hadn't said anything at the time.

"You get distracted easily, don't you?" She'd beamed on one occasion from behind her desk. "Are you sure you don't want some help?"

Miss Moonlight

She'd asked Harry that question a lot over the years, but he would always just shake his head and that would usually be the end of that. Things would then continue as they always had before until their next meeting but, in his last year at Redbricks, something had happened to change all that.

Illustration by David Axtell.

The truth was, something — or rather someone — had happened that changed everything. It had been in the same draughty hall that he'd first had the clue that his life was about to change so dramatically. The headmistress had announced during one morning assembly that Mrs Hayes, the art teacher, was having to take early retirement and that a new art teacher would be joining the school within the next week or two.

Harry hadn't taken much notice at the time. After all, what difference could a new art teacher make to him?

But he'd been wrong. In fact, as he found out, Harry had never been so wrong about anything in his whole life.

And it was Miss Moonlight who had made all the difference. The magical, wonderful Miss Moonlight.

Harry was listening to Miss Moonlight right now. He always listened to Miss Moonlight, hanging on every single word. He thought he could listen to her sparkly voice for hours.

Harry had never imagined that an ordinary voice could be sparkly before he met her. Eyes, yes. But a voice? Then again, Miss Moonlight was far from being an ordinary teacher.

Miss Moonlight taught art, and Harry couldn't imagine her ever doing anything else. She was perfect for the job. Sometimes it was hard even to remember the old art teacher, Mrs Hayes, because Miss Moonlight seemed always to have been there.

She was so different from the prim and proper Mrs Hayes, who told them all to sit still and be quiet. Miss Moonlight, on the other hand, moved round the classroom in her floaty dresses as if she was doing a hypnotic dance.

Always busy, hanging up streamers and her pupils' work, she reminded him of a bird making her nest.

She was just like that magpie at the bottom of his gran's garden — and Harry and the other pupils were the chicks that hadn't quite learned to fly on their own yet.

Harry looked around at his classmates, spread over the school field like patches of mushrooms on the grass. He was in his usual place, leaning against the oak tree in the corner, sunlight dappled around him.

Miss Moonlight liked to take classes outside. She said it was important to keep in touch with nature — not like Mrs Hayes, who would draw the blinds and close the windows in an attempt to eliminate all distractions and get them to pay attention.

Harry watched a spider crawl over his hand and made himself look at what he'd done so far.

Miss Moonlight had told them to do a piece of "art from the heart", one of her favourite sayings. By that she meant anything that captured their interest, or that meant something to them. They could draw it, paint or just write about it — whatever they liked.

Harry had found that his interest in art blossomed under Miss Moonlight. She didn't turn her nose up and tut the way Mrs Hayes had when he drew exciting scenes from the "Star Wars" films.

She simply pointed out that he might use a bit more perspective to make the figures in the background more distant, or try doing the drawing as a painting so that he could use really dramatic colours.

She never discouraged any of his ideas and Harry found that he was trying harder to please her because she asked so little of him.

THE blank piece of paper in front of Harry seemed to be mocking him. He'd been staring at it for the best part of half an hour now. The problem was that there were just too many ideas swirling around his head.

Autumn trees, puppies, crashing waves — he could do those any time. Today, he wanted it to be special. Not only was this the last art lesson, it was the last ever lesson at Redbricks.

It seemed more than a special occasion — to him it was momentous. And he wanted to commemorate it with something suitable.

Harry wanted to draw something special for Miss Moonlight so she'd have something to remember him by when he'd gone.

He had so much to tell her. How could he say it all on a single sheet of A4 paper? Miss Moonlight was the best teacher he'd ever had. She hadn't just taught him art, she'd opened his eyes to a whole new world.

It had been thanks to her that he'd realised that, if he focused his thoughts, and kept his imagination on a leash until he got into the art room, he could do things he'd never dreamed of before.

Whether it was sums in Maths or sentences in English, she'd made Harry feel he could do anything.

As the amount of meetings with the headmistress dropped, other teachers started to respond to Harry, too. He wasn't such an "under-retriever" after all. In fact, he'd hardly been sent to see the headmistress at all in the last six months.

Well, apart from that time he'd got into a fight because another boy had said Miss Moonlight turned into a werewolf at midnight. Harry still got angry when he thought about that.

How could anyone say anything nasty about Miss Moonlight? She was the prettiest lady he'd ever seen. The whole room lit up when she walked in and smiled at you.

HARRY?" The sparkly voice startled him.

Somehow she'd managed to walk across the field without him even realising.

"Hello, miss."

Miss Moonlight looked down at his blank piece of paper.

"No ideas? You're usually on your fifth piece of paper by now." She laughed and Harry thought, as he always did, that she had a beautiful laugh.

"I can't decide what to do."

"Oh, I see." She glanced over at the other pupils dotted around, heads bowed. "I bet you can't wait to get to secondary school, can you, Harry?"

And, despite all the promises he'd made to himself to keep his feelings secret, Harry found himself shaking his head.

"I like Redbricks. I like being at the top of the school. And now everything's going to be different. I'm going to be the lowest of the low again." He looked up for a moment. "New teachers, too. Ones who don't know me . . ."

Miss Moonlight kneeled down on the grass beside him, not caring about her rose-patterned skirt getting dirty.

"And I thought you were one of those people who never got scared of anything. I guess change makes us all nervous." She paused in contemplation. "I'll never forget my first day here."

Harry looked at her.

"Were you nervous?"

"Scared out of my wits, more like! For the first week I kept losing my pen and it turned out it was behind my ear every time!" She grinned.

"But, if I remember correctly, it was the last lesson on a Friday afternoon when a nice young man came up to me.

"He shook my hand, wished me good luck and said that it would take a while to fit in, but everything would turn out OK."

Harry was blushing.

"And do you know what? That moment has stayed with me ever since. Whenever I get all het up over something, I think about it, smile and stop worrying. I've always meant to thank you for that, Harry."

SHE lifted her hand and for a moment it hung there, waiting. Then Harry's fingers joined with hers and they shook firmly, a proper businessman's handshake.

"You're a brilliant artist, Harry. I hope you know that, because it's true. And we all get worried about change — but unfortunately that's what life is all about. Usually everything does turn out OK, though — just like you said."

She stood up and their hands pulled apart.

"Just don't forget to send me an invitation to your shows when you're famous, will you? I can't wait."

Harry watched Miss Moonlight walk away, each step perfect, rust-coloured hair floating in the breeze. He watched her until she sat down beside the nearest cluster of pupils, then he picked up his pencil, knowing exactly what he had to do.

* * * *

A little later Harry smiled, looking back at Redbricks Primary School as an already fading memory. He wondered if Miss Moonlight had found the picture yet.

He'd slipped it beneath her classroom door before he left. He hoped she liked it; he had a feeling she would.

It was as she'd walked away that the idea had struck him. It was the perfect way to show Miss Moonlight exactly how much she meant to him.

His picture was of a mother magpie tending her nest as she watched her chick taking off on his first solo flight into the world.

But the mother magpie wasn't sad, and neither was the chick. In fact, they were smiling, because they both knew that this first flight was meant to happen, that moving on was all part of life — and that it was the right thing for both of them.

And something else — they both knew in their hearts that this wasn't the end, but simply the beginning of a bright new future. ■

Taking The Plunge

by Jo Thomas.

Illustration by Mark Viney.

JOAN'S stomach somersaulted as she looked over the edge at the drop below her. The ground was such a long way down!

When she realised everything had started spinning in front of her, she pulled back sharply and closed her eyes, fighting down a surge of panic.

What on earth was she doing here? How could she ever have thought she'd be able to go through with it? She was shaking with nerves already, and this was just the practice fall!

"It's no good — I'll never manage the real jump if the ground's moving in front of my eyes already!" Joan whispered to Gerald as they stood halfway up a ladder, inside the large aeroplane hangar. Somewhere, in the distance, she heard the young instructor telling them to keep their legs together and look up, as the group took it in turns to jump off the box.

"You'll be fine, honestly. I was just the same on my first jump, but look at me now — a seasoned jumper!" Gerald laughed, his silver-grey head nodding encouragingly.

Joan wasn't convinced. She looked down at her all-in-one boiler suit and the straps and harness that she was wearing with a sense of disbelief.

She'd be sixty-three tomorrow, and here she was about to fling herself out of a plane. She must be out of her mind!

"Next," the instructor shouted.

She felt a little nudge, and turned to look at the smiling Gerald.

"He's calling yo-ou!"

Joan snapped herself out of her daydream and back to the situation in hand. She'd agreed to jump out of a plane and she needed to know how to do it properly.

She stepped up to jump off the box. Her stomach flipped over and came up to meet her throat, but she remembered to keep her feet together as she jumped.

* * * *

"Right, everyone, you're all set, so let's get you into the plane." The instructor smiled. "Well done, everybody — and good luck!"

The small crowd clapped and a couple of people whooped. Joan tried to join in but somehow she couldn't get her hands to do what her brain was telling them.

Gerald looked at her and, sensing her apprehension, put his arm round her shoulders, gave it a little squeeze and directed her out of the hangar. They stepped out into bright sunshine and Joan could smell the sun on hot tarmac.

"Wait, Joan, we have a few minutes. Let's take a seat." A calm voice spoke in her ear.

Joan allowed herself to be guided by Gerald towards a nearby low wall. She realised she was feeling shivery and tearful and grappled in her pocket for a tissue to blow her nose.

"Oh, Joan, love. Don't get upset! It's not worth it . . ." Gerald took hold of both her hands.

"If you don't want to do it," he said, moving as close as he could to her, "then don't do it. It's just a charity parachute jump — no-one's going to force you to go through with it."

"Just nerves getting the better of me." Joan gave her nose a final blow, then sat up straight, stuffing the soggy tissue back into her pocket.

"No, Gerald, a parachute jump is what I signed up for, and that's what I'm going to do. I'm not going to let down all those people who've sponsored me." She managed a brave smile.

"That's my girl." He gave her hand another little squeeze and they sat in companionable silence, watching the rest of the group making their way towards the plane.

"It's been quite a year, hasn't it?" Gerald mused.

"It certainly has!" Joan managed a laugh, her nerves still settling.

"Who'd have thought a quiet cup of coffee in town would have led to me sitting here with a parachute strapped to my back?"

THEY'D met nearly a year ago, when Joan had decided to stop off in Giglio's café, after dropping off her mother's library books. Gerald had been putting up posters for a church fête and he'd spilled his coffee. Joan had come to the rescue with napkins and a supply of tissues from her handbag.

Over another cup of milky coffee, Gerald had told her all about the fête. He'd volunteered to organise it but there had been all sorts of snags.

They'd been trying to build a coconut shy — but he'd only been able to buy seven coconuts in the local supermarket.

And "guess the weight of the pig" was turning into a hazardous occupation, because Gertie refused to be separated from her pal, Daisy. He'd just redesigned the banner to "guess the weight of the pigs —"

"You certainly keep busy," Joan said when she stopped laughing.

It was only then that she realised what a long time it had been since she'd laughed.

Caring for her mother had kept her busy for a number of years, but now that Mum was in a residential home, Joan found herself trying to fill her days with cleaning, washing and shopping for the smallest items that could really have waited until the next time she went out.

"How does your wife put up with you spending all your time being chief fête organiser?" she asked, still smiling.

"My wife died a few years ago," Gerald answered more quietly than Joan was expecting.

"Oh, I'm terribly sorry." Joan felt embarrassed at her own thoughtlessness.

"Please — don't be." Gerald smiled. "She was a wonderful woman. She was the one who made me realise that life is for living.

"Before she died, she made me promise to make the most of every day. It was her gift to me . . . so that's what I do. I fund-raise for the church. I went to Italian classes and then I took up parachute jumping — something I've always wanted to do.

"So, how about you? Do you have any children?" Gerald had asked.

"Just the one daughter, Louise." Joan smiled. "And now a granddaughter, Isabelle."

"Ah, lovely . . ."

The Little Girl

Jessica Jane is
out for fun,
Such a fortunate
girl, it's plain,
So snug and warm,
from top to toe,
What matter if the
cold winds blow?
She clapped her hands
when she saw the snow,
"Hooray!" cried Jessica Jane.

Pulling her little toboggan along,
That Papa made, with such flair,
To Market Square her way she'll wend,
To buy hot chestnuts from our friend,
For Jessica Jane has twopence to spend,
And Charlie stands smiling there . . .

"Hallo, Jessica Jane!" cries he,
For a favourite customer is she,
Who always has a moment to spare
To caress little Pip, who is hovering there.

— Kathleen O'Farrell.

"Yes . . . Louise's father — I mean, my husband — well, ex-husband, left when my daughter started secondary school." Joan surprised herself at her own openness.

"He ran off with the women's captain from the badminton club. She was ten years younger than me."

Joan grinned.

"Or so she said!" she added and they both giggled.

From that moment on, they'd been firm friends.

JOAN, I've been meaning to say something for a while," Gerald began nervously, cutting across Joan's thoughts. "I've really enjoyed this past year."

"Me, too." She gave his hand a little squeeze. "After Derek left I was so busy being a mum and holding down a job, I never had time for anything else. I'd forgotten how to be just me."

"That's all changed now." Gerald grinned as she smiled back.

"It was difficult to adjust to not being needed at first. When Louise had Isabelle, I offered to look after her when she went back to work. I said I'd sell the house and move closer to them, but she told me there was a crèche at work.

"Then Mum became ill, and I was kept busy caring for her. But after that, when she had to go into the home . . . well, to be honest, I felt redundant."

Gerald nodded understandingly.

"It was something Mum said that brought me to my senses, in the end," Joan went on. "It was a beautiful, sunny day just like this and I was taking her for a walk around the gardens at the home. She told me she felt like a bird in a cage.

"She'd always been so fit before her illness — and now, well, it was then I realised just how quickly life passes by. How quickly Louise had grown up and made her own life. She didn't need me in the same way any more. It's only natural. I understand that now."

Gerald put a comforting hand on her shoulder.

"It was when Louise told me I should 'get a life.' It really hurt." She cringed at the memory. "All I could see was her getting on with her busy life and me being left behind."

She smiled at Gerald.

"I was lost. I wasn't a mother any more. And Mum didn't need me to look after her. Louise was right — I was trying to live my life through hers. I wasn't a wife — or a carer any more. I had nothing left. I just didn't know how to live for myself any more.

"If only she'd known what she'd started!" She gestured at her parachute harness. "I don't think this is quite what she meant by 'get a life'!"

"Joan, I was lost, too," Gerald said quietly. "I was so wrapped up in trying to keep busy, trying to hide from my feelings, doing charity work, that I wasn't living life. I was hiding from everything. It's you who's helped me move on."

Before she could reply, the instructor's voice broke into their thoughts.

"OK, you two? Whenever you're ready." He smiled encouragingly. "The conditions are perfect for this jump."

Joan took a deep breath and Gerald watched her face. She gave him a wobbly smile and they stood up together, heading towards the plane, hand in hand.

Their friendship had begun when she'd visited the fête. Then they'd shared the odd coffee, and she'd helped with his charity whist drives, and they'd enjoyed the occasional Sunday roasts together.

Life had bobbed along quite easily for the two of them. Neither had admitted just how fond they were becoming of each other, and both, she was sure, were afraid of taking the next step. Where would it lead them?

Inside the plane, there was an excited buzz of chatter as everyone strapped themselves into their seats, under the watchful eye of the instructor.

The engines gave a roar, and as the plane began to move along the runway, swiftly picking up speed, Joan clung on to the bars at her side and stared at Gerald, panic in her eyes. He held her other hand tight and didn't let go of her.

"You'll be all right. You'll love it." Gerald shouted above the engine noise. "This is a new beginning. It's time you did something for you." He took a deep breath. "And time I stopped living in the past."

"I don't know." Joan's nerves suddenly took hold of her again. "I'm an old woman, for goodness' sake. What am I doing?"

"Living!" Gerald shouted back above the din as the instructor opened the side door.

"How on earth did I end up agreeing to do this?" Joan shouted.

"Because you love me?" He laughed, standing up as the instructor beckoned him forward.

JOAN looked at him and this time her racing heartbeat had nothing to do with nerves. She'd vowed never to get involved with another man again. And she hadn't, not for nineteen years — until now, she realised, in surprise.

"You know, Gerald," she said to him as she stood in the open doorway, "I think you might be right."

"Make the jump, Joan. Trust me. I just want to make you happy." He put his hand to his mouth, then blew her a kiss.

"What, by making me throw myself out of a plane?" she joked back above the roar of the engines.

"I'll be waiting for you."

With a final grin and a wave, Gerald jumped.

The instructor beckoned Joan to come forward for her turn. She stood up shakily and held on tightly to the bar by the door. The wind rushed against her face.

Other jumpers were lining up behind her. She looked at the instructor, who gave her the thumbs up.

She stepped up to the edge and stared down at the graceful parachute floating below.

This time the ground didn't spin quite so much and she could make out the shapes and patterns of the fields and houses below.

"It's beautiful," she shouted.

The instructor smiled reassuringly. Joan wondered what Gerald would do if she didn't jump. No-one would mind, that's what he'd said. She didn't have to do it.

"Oh, yes, you do. You've come this far! Why stop now?" she muttered to herself.

"You OK, Joan?" The instructor was now looking a little concerned.

"Never better." Joan smiled back confidently.

She took a step forward and jumped.

She felt like a bird that had been let out of its cage. She was free and very much alive. The blood pumped round her body. It was the best feeling in the world!

"YEEEE-HAAAH," she yelled as she plunged towards the ground.

JOAN, that was fantastic!" Gerald came running over, now free of his harness, and hugged her.

Joan, looking past his shoulder, was beaming. A small crowd on the edge of the field were clapping and cheering.

Little Isabelle was jumping up and down in excitement, Louise was laughing in delight and Mum — dear old Mum, who'd insisted on being here — was waving frantically from her wheelchair.

She was wrapped up for a cold winter's day, in a blanket and wearing her best hat, in honour of the occasion — and she was grinning like the Cheshire Cat.

Joan turned to Gerald, her eyes shining.

"It was wonderful!"

Gerald put his arm around her shoulder.

"So are you," he said, smiling proudly.

Her eyes filling with happy tears, Joan turned to him and kissed him on the lips. He kissed her back.

Behind them, Joan heard Louise's gasp of surprise.

"Come on," she said, taking Gerald's hand. "Let's go and get on with our life — together." ■

SLIDING quietly out from the warm bed so as not to disturb her sleeping husband, Gill pulled jeans and a sweater over her nightdress, picked up her shoes and tip-toed down the stairs.

She had wakened early so that she could watch the dawn break and the sun slowly rise over the rolling hills and fields which surrounded the farmhouse. This time tomorrow, she and Gordon would be living in a cottage in the nearby village and she wanted to savour every moment of their last morning on Hill Farm.

Walking into the dark kitchen, Gill shivered as her footsteps echoed on the wooden floor. The family had transported most of the furniture and kitchen appliances to the cottage the previous day.

There was now a gaping hole where the old Aga had stood, and the long pine table which had been used for family meals, as well as a surface for cooking and baking, drawing and sewing, had gone to a family friend.

Indeed, everything had gone, either for auction or to the new house, apart from a microwave, the kettle, some crockery and the dog's bowl.

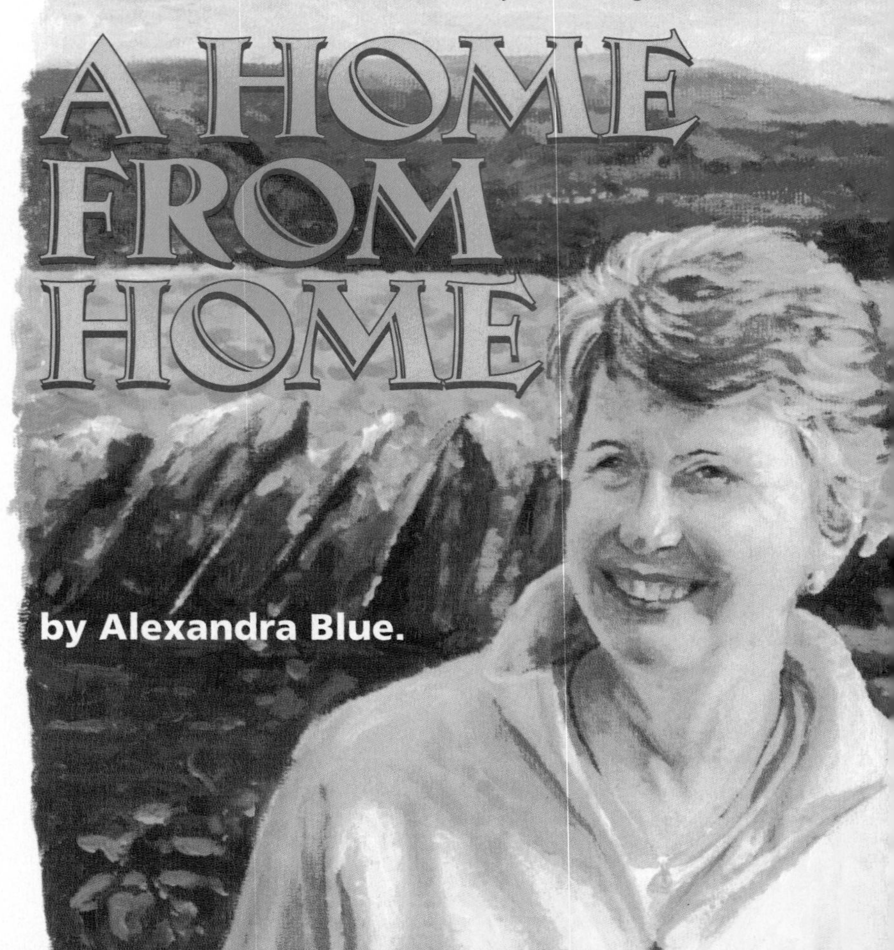

A HOME FROM HOME

by Alexandra Blue.

Just at that, Shep stood up and wagged his tail.

"Hello, doggy," Gill said, tickling his soft ears. "Do you want to watch the sunrise with me?"

Shep snuffled, stretched and trotted after her when she stepped outside into the cool September morning.

"Brrr." Gill grabbed a jacket from the peg by the door. One thing she wouldn't miss when they moved to the village was going out in all weathers to feed cattle or help Gordon with the lambing in the dead of night.

But she would miss the glorious smells of pure country air and freshly ploughed earth. Gill filled her lungs, whistled to the dog and walked across the yard to the small paddock where their daughter, Rosie, had once kept her pony.

She smiled at the memory of Rosie riding bareback round the field, her hair flowing out behind her as she cantered fearlessly in circles or figures of eight.

She had loved that pony but, with the contrariness of youth, the moment

Illustration by David Young.

she became interested in boys and fashion, Rosie had lost interest in riding.

The pony was now being cared for by the children on the next farm and was still going strong. But Gill found herself wondering if she, too, would lose interest in farming and animals when they moved to the village . . .

NEITHER she nor Gordon particularly wanted to leave. They were "still-fit-at-fifty", and Rossie Farm had belonged to Gordon's family for over a hundred years. But it had been losing money for a long time. They had no sons to hand the farm on to, and so Gordon had decided that they should cut their losses, buy a place in the village to be closer to Rosie and the grandchildren, and find themselves "proper" jobs.

Gill smiled. She had already started working as a care assistant at the primary school and loved it. Gordon was to help out at the local mart.

They would have regular income and hours of leisure time now that they didn't have the responsibility of acres of land and hundreds of sheep and cows to care for.

The darkness was fading, the sky turning to pale grey with streaks of silver. The moon still shone. She could hear something rustling in a gorse bush.

The future might look bright, but she was going to miss the special peace that you found living on a farm, the feeling of being at one with nature.

Yet it didn't sound the way it should. There was no lowing of cattle. She couldn't hear the distinctive bleating from the sheep on the hill, and the cockerel hadn't given his early morning wake-up call.

Not that she should be surprised. They had gradually sold off the livestock over the last few weeks, as well as most of the land. But at least she could take comfort in knowing that the new owners planned to renovate the farmhouse and turn it into a family home and guesthouse for hikers. It was good to know that the old place would bring pleasure to lots of people . . .

The sky was now egg-shell blue. Gill waited for her first glimpse of the sun behind the dark hills.

"I thought you'd be here," Gordon said, walking over the yard to join her.

She smiled at him.

"Our last morning on Rossie Farm."

"Soon to be our first night in the cottage. We'll be fine, Gill."

"I know," she said, leaning against his strong, wiry body. "But I will miss the place. There are so many memories . . ."

He nodded.

"Remember that time you drove the tractor and crashed into the stable door?"

Gill giggled.

"I wasn't much of a tractorman — woman," she corrected hastily.

They laughed together. She felt his lips on her hair.

"We'll have more time for each other," Gordon said, as if wanting to share the list of advantages which he'd compiled when they decided to sell.

"We've never been able to go away to a hotel for the weekend like other people, or take off to the sun for a week. The farm always tied us down."

"And we'll be able to afford a proper car that doesn't break down every ten miles like that old faithful," she added, pointing to their decrepit Ford.

They laughed again but grew silent when the first rays of the sun shimmered behind the hill.

"Isn't it beautiful?" Gill whispered, watching a tiny slit of yellow appear and grow brighter and bigger.

"Perfect," Gordon said.

"I'll miss the views we get up here."

"You'll still get a nice view from the village."

She hadn't thought of that. They had a long, secluded garden behind the cottage with grass, a vegetable plot, apple and plum trees and two potting sheds. There was no reason why she couldn't walk down the garden of a morning and watch the sun begin its gradual ascent.

"We'll be fine," she said, repeating his statement from minutes before.

"Of course we will," Gordon agreed. "Now, any chance of some breakfast?"

Gill reached up for a kiss.

"I'll fetch some fresh eggs."

Then she stopped, her eyes filling with sudden tears. She had kept hens throughout the thirty years of her marriage, had sold the eggs to the village shop, and enjoyed every minute of talking to her "chooks", as she called them, listening to their contented clucking as they scratched and pecked in the farmyard.

But her hens had gone, taken away by the neighbours the previous day.

"Oh, Gordon," she said, searching in her pocket for a handkerchief. "I don't want to move."

"I know, I know," he soothed, squeezing her hand. "It will be a wrench. But we're doing the right thing, Gill. Believe me."

"How can you be sure? I love my home and I'm missing my chooks already!"

"Gill, stop it!" He gave her a shake. "The house is old, draughty and in need of a new roof. Even the henhouse is a sorry sight! We *have* to move."

She looked over at the farmhouse. Weeds sprouted from the chimney-pot, the window frames were rotting and paint was flaking from the outside walls. Then she turned her attention to the dilapidated henhouse with straw poking out of the gaps in the wood.

She sniffed and wiped her eyes. He was right. They did have to move. And the hens would be happier in their new watertight home at the neighbouring farm.

But she would miss the fresh eggs and the joy of watching baby chicks running about the yard in the spring sunshine. She would miss everything about Hill Farm . . .

BY early afternoon, the rest of their belongings had been transported to the cottage, Gill had finished cleaning the farmhouse and Shep was sitting on the doorstep, waiting patiently for his master to return.

Gill put her rubber gloves and cloth in a bucket and checked the time. Where was Gordon? He should have been back ages ago.

She knew that their daughter had made lunch for them at the cottage. But at this rate, the soup would be burned and the sandwiches curled up at the edges.

Shading her eyes from the sun, Gill looked down the farm road.

"Here he comes," she said, waving when she recognised the car bumping over the pot holes. "What kept you?"

Gordon climbed out of the driver's seat and bent down to fuss over Shep, who was barking and whining with joy.

Glencoe Hills, Argyllshire

PICTURE-POSTCARD perfect, and one of the most famous glens in Scotland, Glen Coe can be stunningly beautiful. The Three Sisters greet you first — Faith, Hope and Charity — outriders to Argyll's highest mountain, Bidean nam Bian.

Further on are the Big and Little Shepherds of Etive — Buchaille Etive

"We had a bit of difficulty getting the bed upstairs. But everything is in place and Rosie has the lunch all ready."

"Good," Gill said. "I'm starving."

Gordon seemed surprised.

"You've cheered up!"

She shrugged. She didn't tell him that she had vacuumed and dusted each

Mor and Buchaille Etive Beag. The sheer 1200-foot cliffs that drop from the Big Shepherd's summit are daunting and well worth a photograph or two.

Not that climbers are put off, however, as these hills are among the most popular in Scotland. Don't worry if you aren't a hillwalker or a climber, though — the magnificent scenery can be enjoyed without having to leave the road!

room of the house with tears running down her face as the memories had swept her back in time.

She had remembered her first night as a married woman in the big bedroom which looked down the glen, and bringing baby Rosie home from the hospital to the nursery which Gordon had decorated.

She had remembered the magic and excitement of Christmas mornings, Hogmanay parties with the neighbours all squeezed into the cosy living-room, and tried to put faces to the hundreds of people she had provided meals for over the years in the big, sunny kitchen, the friends and family, farm labourers, tractor salesmen, hill walkers . . .

"I've said goodbye to the house," she said, locking the door for the last time. "I'm ready to go."

Gordon's eyes were concerned.

"We could come back later for a last look over the place before handing the keys to the solicitor?"

Gill shook her head and managed a wobbly smile. She had a new home and a new life. It was time to move on.

When they reached the cottage, Rosie and her husband were waiting to welcome them. Gill kissed them both and laughed when she spotted her grandchildren carefully sliding down the spiral staircase on their bottoms.

"We want stairs like yours, Gran," six-year-old Connor said. "They're great!"

Gill grinned.

"Now that we're living next door to each other you can come here and play on the stairs any time."

"Don't say that," Rosie hissed, blue eyes twinkling. "They might invite all their friends! Are you ready for lunch, Mum?"

"In a minute," Gill said, admiring the pretty lounge with its terracotta painted walls, pine panelled doors and low ceilings. Rosie had lit the wood burning stove and hung the curtains and it was so warm and homely that Gill felt quite overwhelmed.

"Thanks for all your help, love. It feels like home already."

Rosie looked pleased.

"It's a lovely cottage. And it'll be much easier to heat and clean than that big cold farmhouse."

GILL smiled and walked into the narrow kitchen. A pot of soup was simmering on the cooker. Her spice jars were lining the worktop. The big brown teapot was sitting by the kettle.

"It even smells like home," she said, giving the soup a stir.

Gordon appeared in the doorway.

"So the cottage smells like home and feels like home. All we need now is for it to *sound* like home." And he pushed open the back door and gave Gill a cheeky grin.

She frowned. What was he playing at? Surely he hadn't arranged for a herd of cows to tramp across the lawn.

Then her ears pricked up as she recognised the distinctive cluck-cluck-cluck, and she brushed past Gordon and into the garden.

"I don't believe it," she gasped, gazing in wonder at the big brown hens scratching the rough ground at the bottom of the garden. "Are they my chooks?"

"Of course," Gordon said proudly. "I retrieved half a dozen of them from the neighbouring farm this morning, made a home for them in the potting shed and built a run with chicken wire. I don't see any reason why we can't keep a few hens. And the neighbours aren't likely to object," he added, looking to Rosie for confirmation.

She giggled.

"You can keep us sweet by giving us eggs now and again. Oh, Mum, what's wrong?" she asked, when Gill burst into tears.

"Nothing," Gill said, crying and laughing at the same time. "I'm just so happy. I really didn't want to leave Hill Farm this morning. There were so many memories. But being here in this lovely new house, with my family next door, my chooks in the garden, and my wonderful, thoughtful husband by my side . . ." She slipped an arm around Gordon and smiled up at him. "What more could I ask for?" ■

SEEING THE LIGHT

by Marion McKinnon.

IF it's Wednesday, it must be art class, Kate thought as she dashed into her flat. She dropped her briefcase in the tiny hall and took her supermarket bag through to the kitchen. Dinner — a rather small ocean pie — went into the microwave. While it slowly

Illustration by Stephanie Axtell.

revolved she grabbed a glass of water and dashed rapidly around the plants, dampening the parched soil.

She must have forgotten to do it yesterday. Tuesdays were such a rush.

Still three minutes on the microwave, so she hurried through to the bedroom and quickly changed her smart skirt suit for a loose pair of jeans and a casual sweater. She tugged a hairbrush through her honey-blonde, practical bob and frowned at herself in the mirror.

I must fit in a haircut next week, she thought. Maybe Thursday. If she skipped dinner there would just be time between work and her aerobics class.

She hurried through to the kitchen and ate her ready meal straight out of its tray, leafing through the morning paper she hadn't got around to reading before leaving for work.

The tray went into the bin, fork still inside. Blast. She scrabbled on hands and knees for a few moments, retrieved the fork, and glanced at her watch. Six-forty. She'd never get there on time!

A dab of lipstick, check the mascara. It would do. Grabbing her purse from the front pocket of her briefcase, she hurried out of the door, one arm still fighting its way into her jacket.

She was late. And for the first class, too.

The harassed-looking woman on the registration desk was arguing with another latecomer who, by the sound of things, was trying to register for a class that had happened last night, but she paused long enough to point Kate to the furthest wing of the Adult Education College.

She found the right classroom just as the door opened and people began to stream out. She looked at her watch in confusion. Seven-ten.

"I haven't missed it, have I?"

Someone laughed.

"Not much to miss," a girl told her. "Tutor's the tall guy in the green shirt. Name's Simon. Ask him."

WHEN they had all left the room Kate went in. She saw a sandy-haired man in his early thirties standing at the front of the room. He was half-facing the blackboard, a chalk duster in his hand.

Kate assumed he was about to erase the equations that covered the board, presumably from a previous class, but as she watched she realised he wasn't moving.

He stood frozen for some seconds, and then very carefully put down the eraser, picked up a piece of chalk and began to add lines to a large number 2. Kate stepped closer and watched in amazement as he transformed it into an impressively accurate caricature of Tony Blair.

Without meaning to, she began to applaud.

He looked round, startled. His eyes were a remarkable shade of emerald green and seemed very wide open, as though he was seeing twice as much in the world around him as anybody else was.

"Haven't you gone yet?" he said. "You'd better hurry or you'll miss the light."

"I've only just got here," she replied, feeling even more confused. "Where was everyone going?"

"Outside. That's your assignment for the lesson." He pointed to the window. "See that field out there? Go into it and find something interesting. Then look at it."

Kate waited.

"And?"

"Isn't that enough for one lesson?"

"I thought this was a drawing class," she objected.

"It is." He glared at her. "Do you actually want to learn to draw?"

"Yes. That's why I signed up."

"Is it? Or did you just come along because it's Wednesday and there's nothing on the telly?"

"Well, if you're going to be like that —" she began.

He turned away from her and studied his sketch with those wide eyes.

"Go outside and look at something. I'll be down in a minute. If you've got any questions, ask me then. Otherwise, go home and vegetate."

IRRITATED, Kate stomped out of the classroom. She was half inclined to return to the front desk and complain, but perhaps it was her own fault for arriving late. He might have given more detailed instructions to the rest of the class.

She hurried down the stairs and out of the rear entrance, which was marked *Fire Exit Only*.

It opened on to a concrete walkway flanked by a high hawthorn hedge. The paving was damp and mossy, obviously little-used. Off to her right, the last few of her classmates were disappearing through a gate, and she hurried after them.

The field was muddy, and she was glad she had changed into casual clothes and comfortable old trainers.

Two or three of the women were teetering around on heels, complaining loudly, and an older man was examining the sole of his patent leather loafer with a sour expression.

Kate stepped around them and headed cautiously into the calf-length grass, looking around for something she might want to draw.

"This is ridiculous," someone objected loudly. "What are we supposed to be looking at?"

Kate turned around.

"I came late," she said. "Didn't the teacher give you any more instructions?"

"He just said to come out here and find something to look at." The woman waved her hands helplessly. "Like what?"

"There are some blackberries over here," Mr Patent Leather Shoes called.

He had remained close to the gate and was staring intently at a knot of brambles that wound its way through the hedge.

Suppressing the urge to giggle, Kate set off towards a copse of trees at the end of the field. Maybe she would find something away from the buildings.

The class spread itself out across the field, most of the twenty or so students looking rather lost. A couple of people had hunkered down and were staring at something in the grass. Kate wondered how long they were supposed to stay out here.

The class was scheduled to run until nine, but although it was still only early September the nights were drawing in. It would be dark before nine, and the air was already beginning to feel cooler.

She shivered as she stepped out of the evening sunlight and into the shade of the trees. Maybe she should have stayed at home and watched telly after all. She hadn't had a night in for ages.

Big Bands

Glenn Miller

The great trombonist, arranger and bandleader Alton Glenn Miller was born in Iowa in 1904.

His first band, formed in 1937, was a failure, but the following year he created the band which would eventually be one of the most successful and popular in the world.

His arrangement of "Moonlight Serenade", which became his signature tune, was known the world over, and other best-loved hits include "In The Mood" and "Tuxedo Junction".

Glenn Miller starred in two films — "Sun Valley Serenade" (1941) and "Orchestra Wives" (1942).

Having joined the US Army in 1942, he and his service band were travelling to France in 1944 when his aircraft was lost crossing the English Channel, never to be found.

Beneath the trees the grass was damp and there were toadstools growing amongst the roots of a gnarled oak. She squatted awkwardly to look at them and saw that they were half-eaten by worms. A rich smell of rotting leaves rose up to greet her and she wrinkled her nose in disgust.

She glanced back out into the field. There seemed to be fewer students now, and she wondered if some people had given up already. Or perhaps they had found their objects and taken them back inside to draw.

That must, after all, be the aim of the exercise.

* * * *

Kate looked around again, determined to find something. Her eyes were drawn to a little clump of blue flowers nestling in the long grass just beyond the trees' shadows. She went over to look more closely. The flowers were

Pictorial Press.

splashes of vibrant colour against jagged leaves.

She decided they would do nicely.

She reached out to pluck a stem, but as she did so a shadow fell across her and a large, tanned hand reached out to stop her.

"What are you doing?"

She looked up, and saw the teacher — Simon. His face was very close to hers, and he was frowning.

"I thought I'd draw these," she said.

"I didn't say to draw anything. I said to look. Just look."

"I have looked."

"And what did you see?"

"These, but I don't know what they're called. Blue flowers. I like the colour," she added, thinking an artist would be attracted to colour.

"That's a start, I suppose." A half-smile brought unexpected warmth to his eyes. "Keep looking."

"How long for?"

He shrugged.

"You'll know when you're done."

"And then I bring them in and draw them?"

"Why the hurry?" He sighed. "No, today you look. Then you go home."

"But what about the drawing lesson?" she insisted. "That's what I came for."

"How can you draw if you can't see?" he demanded, and stood up. "Learn to see. Then I can teach you to draw."

He walked away, leaving Kate speechless at his rudeness. Then, not sure what else to do, she looked back at the patch of blue flowers and counted their petals: five on each one. The centre of each flower contained a group of tiny stalks, topped in black. The petals themselves were veined with pink.

Her knees were aching and she stood up. There were only three students left in the field. Simon was standing with his back to them all, apparently looking very closely at the bole of an oak tree.

Kate looked back at the little flowers, but there was nothing else to see. She gave up and stomped back across the muddy field. As she reached the gate,

Mr Patent Leather Shoes glanced around from his brambles.

"You, too?" He grinned, showing blackberry-stained teeth.

On her way back through the building, Kate paused at the reception desk.

"Do you have any complaint forms?" she asked.

The woman raised an eyebrow.

"I've got a couple left," she said dryly, and handed one over. Kate filled it in then and there, and stomped off to her car. If the traffic wasn't too bad, she'd catch that late-night detective show after all.

SEVERAL times that week, Kate found a hazy image of little blue flowers drifting across her vision as she tried to concentrate on paperwork. She strove to remember exactly what they had looked like and realised that she had only the vaguest idea.

She began to wonder how much detail it was possible to recall from a scene and took to pausing at random intervals as her attention was snagged by a coffee stain on her colleague's desk or the pattern of frosting on the window in the ladies' loos.

On Friday, she earned herself a stiff reprimand after the staff meeting because she had to be asked twice to begin her presentation. She had been examining the pattern of dandruff on the personnel manager's collar, but didn't feel able to say so.

By Wednesday afternoon, Kate couldn't wait for the art class to begin. When she got home she skipped dinner altogether to save a few minutes. She arrived at college early, and went straight to the field.

The sun was lower than it had been last week, the shadows longer, and she wasn't sure where the little patch of flowers had been. She walked across to the copse of trees and looked back, trying to spot the vivid patch of colour.

It was that way, she thought, and began to walk forward, her eyes scanning the ground.

After a few minutes of wandering around and backtracking, she found a small patch of leaves that looked familiar. Crouching beside the plant, she gently took the few remaining flowerheads into her palm.

Browning petals drooped from withered stalks, and several detached as she touched them. The wonderful blue pigment she remembered was completely gone.

Now I'll never know what they looked like, she thought gloomily as she stared at the withered plant. What was she to do now? She wasn't sure she wanted to draw dead flowers.

"It's always best to look when you have the opportunity," a voice behind her said. "The chances are it won't be there when you come back."

She looked up into Simon's almost-familiar green eyes as he hunkered down beside her.

"I've been trying all week to remember what they looked like," she said. "I thought I saw them last week. I thought I'd looked so carefully, but I couldn't remember for the life of me."

"Frustrating, isn't it?" He nodded. "But it gets easier with practice."

He was looking at her closely, those wide eyes travelling over her face, an active, searching gaze that seemed to see everything of who she was. It was a little unnerving.

"I didn't expect to see you again," he said at last.

"Why? Because I was impatient last week? People can learn, you know."

"I'm glad to hear it. But no, that wasn't the reason. My class has been cancelled."

"Cancelled?" she exclaimed. "Why?"

"There were complaints," he said wryly.

Guiltily, she remembered the form she had filled in so hurriedly on her way out last week. She had been rushing home for something — oh, yes, some far-fetched programme on telly. She couldn't even remember exactly what she had written.

"I'm sorry."

He shrugged.

"I'll approach it differently next time. People need to learn how to see, but first I have to teach them why it's important."

SHE looked at him more closely and saw sadness in the tight lines around his mouth and the curve of his neck.

"I've been looking at things all week," she told him on an impulse. "Not the way you look, I'm sure, but I've been noticing details, things I've walked past a thousand times before.

"I spent half an hour yesterday watching the way the shadow of the blinds moved across the photocopier."

Simon grinned suddenly.

"I'm glad to hear I've had such an effect on your productivity. Just think how it might have plummeted if the class had run."

She smiled and stood up.

"Actually, while my mind was wandering, I had a couple of really good ideas for how to make my training sessions more visually appealing."

"Perhaps I should take up a new career, teaching business seminars!" He laughed.

"Perhaps you should," she said seriously. "It isn't only artists who need to be able to see what's right under their noses."

"How about a deal?" he suggested. "You teach me how to present my ideas in a way that doesn't chase people off, and I'll teach you how to draw."

"I'd like that."

She smiled into his eyes and realised that, for the first time in months, she wasn't in a hurry to be somewhere else. ■

Never Too Late

Illustration by Heidi Spindler.

"DADDY!"

The giggling shriek causes me to turn my head. A red-headed girl, about eight years old and wearing a duffel coat and wellies, is laughing as her father swings her round on the beach.

Annabel never called me Daddy.

The fresh sea air buffets my face, making me pull my coat tighter around me. Although it is a brisk day, the promenade is surprisingly crowded, the beach full of families, children bundled up in coats and scarves, dogs racing madly across the cold, wet sand.

I'm not sure why I agreed to meet Annabel here, except it reminds me of the summer days we used to come here together, just her and me, to share drippy ice-creams and paddle in the waves. Like father and daughter . . . or so I believed.

It was here that I met Tracey. I'd always thought I was a confirmed bachelor, until Annabel stumbled on the promenade and pitched a strawberry ice-cream on to my shirt.

"Oh, heavens! Annabel!" Tracey looked at me in horror.

Annabel stared at me with the guarded curiosity of a shy six-year-old before she realised she no longer had any ice-cream on her cone.

"My ice-cream!" She looked ready to burst into tears.

"Never mind," I said, breaking into a smile. "I'll buy you another one."

"You don't —" Tracey stopped whatever protest she was going to make.

Our eyes met over Annabel's tousled head, and something flickered to life inside me. It was as if, at that moment, I chose to take on a role I had never envisioned for myself . . . a father.

We spent the rest of the afternoon together, and as twilight crept on to the beach, Tracey and I made plans to see each other again.

"I'm sorry about your shirt," she said with a wry grin.

"I'm not." I smiled back. "Look what happened because of it."

•

OUR courtship was whirlwind and chaotic, conducted with Annabel as our chaperone of sorts. Dates were dinners for three at the local pizza place, or walks in the park to feed the ducks.

I worried that Annabel wouldn't accept me. Her father had walked out on her and Tracey when she was a baby. It infuriated me, but it was done. He'd never been in touch, never explained, and Annabel couldn't remember him at all. Several years later Tracey discovered he'd died in a car crash.

"She needs a father," Tracey told me. "Someone to guide her, besides me."

I so wanted to be that father . . . that daddy. Yet I didn't know the first thing about fatherhood. So I remained afraid that I would do something to bring my fragile relationship with Annabel tumbling down like a child's tower of bricks.

I shouldn't have worried, not then. Annabel accepted me with surprising ease. It was as if she'd been waiting for a father, and knew at once that with me she'd found one at last. I remember the first outing we had alone together.

"You'll be fine," Tracey urged me. "The two of you need some bonding time."

Afraid of failing what seemed like a critical test, I did everything I could to win Annabel over . . . a trip to the zoo, ice-creams, lollies, balloons. Looking back, I can see it was the wrong way to go about it.

by Katharine Swartz.

As it was, I returned her overtired and wired on too much sugar, at six o'clock at night. Tracey gave me a bemused look as Annabel raced around the lounge, her hands and face still sticky from the candy floss.

"You had a good time, then?"

"I think so."

Tracey shook her head.

"Annabel wants to be with you, Mike. You don't need to buy her love. Just be yourself — trust your instincts."

Annabel decided to call me Daddy Mike. I was delighted to be called Daddy anything. We seemed like a real family then, the three of us. As we

Illustration by L. Antico.

sat round the table for tea, I'd gaze at Tracey and Annabel's faces and wonder what more a man could want in life.

Then Annabel turned twelve. All of a sudden, this shy girl-child was demanding things like pierced ears, eyeshadow and dates with boys.

I was bewildered by it all, and clearly out of my depth. Even Tracey, who seemed to know it all, struggled with Annabel's tantrums and door slamming.

"I know this is typical teenager behaviour," she said tiredly one evening after Annabel had flounced up to her bedroom. "But honestly, how long is this going to go on?"

OF course, the inevitable happened . . . or it felt like it was inevitable to me. We had a big row, Annabel and I, which was nothing new.

"You can't tell me what to do," Annabel shouted, her face flushed with anger. "You're not my real father, and you never will be!"

The words caused something to freeze within me. Annabel's eyes glittered with malicious victory, as if she sensed the power her simple statement had over me. I hesitated, wondering how to respond.

Any sensible man, I know now, would have told her that was rubbish, that he was her father in every way that mattered. Any sensible man would have seen the glint of insecurity and fear beneath the tantrum, and given her a hug, perhaps told her he'd always be there for her.

Looking back, I know that's what I should have done. At the time, I was too shocked to do anything but step back and shake my head.

"No, I'm not," I said quietly.

Annabel stared at me, shocked by my admission, and slammed the door. Feeling as if I'd just made the situation even worse, I retreated downstairs.

I can't be sure, of course, but I think that was the turning point in our relationship. Any pretensions I had of being Annabel's father began to slip away. I allowed them to slip, out of sheer helplessness.

The "Daddy" dropped from my name, so I was just "Mike". Every time we had a row, Annabel reminded me of the one thing I couldn't change. Every time it cut me to the quick.

Tracey tried to encourage me, and she always stood beside me. That seemed to infuriate Annabel more. Perhaps she remembered the days when it had just been her and Tracey, perhaps she felt like we were ganging up on her.

Whatever it was, and whatever we tried, nothing seemed to work. It was as if the few precious years of innocence, when I'd felt like her true father and she'd accepted me as such, had never been.

As Annabel matured into an adult, our relationship entered a neutral, emotionless zone. The tirades of her teenage years had subsided, and she'd become an accomplished and friendly young woman I wanted to be proud of, if she'd let me.

When Annabel was twenty-two she brought home Stuart, her

almost-fiancé. It occurred to me then, as I shook his hand, how unfatherly I had become.

I had slipped out of it completely, almost without realising. I'd allowed myself to take a step back, afraid of being rejected again. No vetting the boyfriends for me, no insisting on less make-up and longer skirts for my little girl. I simply stood there, smiling politely and nodding my head.

We threw a small party when Annabel and Stuart became engaged. Champagne and hors d'oevres for twenty close friends.

Somehow I ended up alone in the kitchen with Annabel. I was taking a tray of mini sausage rolls out of the oven, she was coming in for a refill.

"Hello, Annabel." Silence yawned between us, and I tried to fill it. "Stuart seems like a nice fellow. A very nice fellow indeed."

"Thank you." Her reply was, as usual, the minimum required.

"I just want to say . . ." I cleared my throat, fumbling for words. "I know things haven't always been easy between us, but I am happy for you."

There was so much more I would've liked to say — to tell her we could have had so much — that I could have been her father, her real father . . . if only she'd let me!

Perhaps if I hadn't been afraid, nervous, unwilling to believe that all parents, whenever they assume that role, experience struggles and doubts . . . perhaps then we would have had a chance at a real relationship.

All this, I knew, came years too late, and so I didn't say anything. I just smiled and hoped that some of my sincerity and regret reached her.

For a moment I thought I saw something in her eyes, some nameless feeling that showed me she still cared. But then it was gone.

AND now I stand here, freezing to death and wondering if Annabel will even show up. She rang me out of the blue, asked me if we could talk privately. I suggested this promenade, sentimental fool that I am.

I turn, as if I can sense Annabel coming, and she is walking down the promenade, her head lowered against the wind. She looks up and waves.

"Hi, Mike. Thanks for meeting me."

"Any time, Annabel. You know that."

We gaze at each other and she slowly nods.

"Yes, I guess I do."

Annabel looks at me directly, half challenging, half afraid, as defiant and tremulous as when she was nine.

"I want to apologise. I've made things worse between us than they need be."

This really takes the wind out of my sails.

"I've always wanted things to be better between us," I say. I pause, then plunge ahead recklessly.

"You might not remember, but we used to come here, to this promenade. The two of us. We had some good times once, when you were little. I helped

Pip

I'm just a wee dog — a wee nuisance, some say,
For I'm always getting in somebody's way.
Charlie's my owner, though if truth be told,
I followed him home once, all hungry and cold,
And when he discovered that I was a stray,
The kind-hearted chap could not turn me away.

And now we're good comrades, real partners are we,
Though there's just one issue where we disagree . . .

I don't care at all for these chestnuts we sell.
Wouldn't nice, juicy sausages do just as well?
Or some jolly old bones, with the marrow inside?
Though I never go hungry, whatever betide,
For when we get home, we're as snug as can be,
And Charlie, my hero, shares supper with me.

— Kathleen O'Farrell.

you learn how to swim."

I don't expect my words to have any effect. But this time is different. This time Annabel's face crumples, and she suddenly begins to cry.

Out of instinct I wrap my arms around her.

"I'm sorry," she says. "I never cry . . . it's just . . ."

"What?" I ask gently.

"I remember." She dashes at the tears on her cheeks, as if she's ashamed of them. "I know I was horrid to you, Mike. It seemed like all my friends' parents were getting divorced. Kids at school said you'd be gone . . . And it had happened before."

"I know I don't remember my real father, but I know he walked out on us. And I was afraid . . . afraid you would leave. I was angry, too, and when I wanted to put things right, it seemed like it was impossible. Then I decided you didn't care, and so neither did I."

SHE says the last bit quietly, but the words seem to echo inside my head. Guilt and regret wash through me.

"I've always cared, Annabel. I should have told you so." I shake my head. "I wish we'd had this talk a long time ago."

"Maybe we weren't ready for it then." Annabel gives me a wobbly smile. "I wasn't easy to get along with."

"And I was too easy to get along with," I say, the realisation coming to me just now.

"There's nothing we can do about the past," Annabel says quietly. "But there is the future."

She pauses, smiling tremulously.

"I wanted to ask you if you'd walk me down the aisle at my wedding. I know we haven't had the best relationship but you've been the only father I've ever had and . . ." she trails off uncertainly ". . . and I'd like you to."

For a moment I am speechless . . . stunned, and filled with hope.

"I'd be honoured."

We smile at each other, foolishly. We've lost so much, so many years. But I'm not going to think about them any more. I'm not going to look back. There's a way forward now, a chance. Perhaps now Annabel will be a real daughter to me . . . and I'll be a real father to her.

"Fancy an ice-cream?" I ask and Annabel smiles almost shyly.

"Why not?"

As we walk down the promenade I see the father with the little red-headed girl. She is dancing around him, chattering. Our gazes meet and he rolls his eyes in the universal expression of the shared joys and trials of fatherhood.

I smile back and nod. He thinks I'm Annabel's father, I realise.

I look at Annabel, walking beside me, and suddenly I know that's what I've always been. I'm still her dad. Nothing can change that. ■

Davey's Dream

Illustration by Brown.

by Barbara Povey.

DAVEY JOHNSTONE sat on a tussock of grass high above Aimsty Cove and hugged his knees. Far below, gentle waves lapped at the golden sand, and out at sea a small yacht tacked to and fro in the freshening breeze.

It would all have been perfect if Dad had been here, but unfortunately Dad was part of a jigsaw of happy memories — before the accident. Now it was just the two of them, him and Mum, trying hard to build a new life on their own.

Davey had become used to having tea at Gran's each day after school, and waiting for Mum to pick him up on her way home from the office. It was a new routine, but he didn't mind it that much. And then it had all changed again — when his mum met Richard.

If Davey was being absolutely truthful, Richard was not a bad guy. The problem was that he seemed, more and more, to be easing into the space in Davey's life which had been Dad's. And no-one could ever take Dad's place.

For as long as he could remember, Davey had longed for a brother. A brother to share in his games and adventures; in fact, share everything. He'd never told anyone this, of course, because it was his secret dream.

He thought his dad must have sensed it, though, because he was always ready to join in roller-skating, ten-pin bowling or canoeing. Dad had worn jeans and trainers, sweatshirts and anoraks. And he'd promised to teach Davey to sail. Dad had been an action man!

RICHARD, on the other hand, always seemed to be wearing a suit. And though he was willing to play chess, or go to the pictures, he didn't really have much in common with a twelve-year-old boy.

Davey had to admit, however, that the tickets for the match at Old Trafford had been an inspired birthday present. He'd pinched himself to make sure he wasn't dreaming when his favourite players emerged from the tunnel.

Of course Mum must have told Richard that Manchester United was his favourite team. In fact, he would bet that the Old Trafford visit must have been her idea. The only thing missing from the perfect day was that his dad wasn't there.

Davey rubbed his knuckles into eyes which had suddenly become misty, and a lone seagull wheeled and shrieked at him.

It's all right for you, he thought gloomily. You're not waiting for Stephanie to arrive. And the frown on his forehead deepened as he thought of the impending disaster. He'd spent his whole life longing for a brother and then Mum had told him that Richard had a daughter, who was away at university. He'd never actually met her, but now she was going to be joining them at the cottage for their summer vacation.

How unlucky could one boy get? And if Mum and Richard should marry, he would end up with Stephanie for a step-sister!

He looked down at the cove again where two girls lay on beach towels, glistening with sun tan oil and doing absolutely nothing. Typical, he thought. Girls were just boring, that was all there was to it.

"Davey!" Mum was calling from the cottage, which was tucked away in a fold of the cliff, almost invisible from where he was sitting. "Davey, will you collect the bread from the bakery, please? I have to go into town to get something for tea . . ."

The breeze tried to whip her words away, but Davey understood.

"OK," he yelled back.

"We won't be long. Stay out of the water while we're away — and be careful." She waved before taking Richard's arm as they climbed the steep steps to the headland.

In her summer dress, with her hair loose and windblown, even Davey had to admit that Mum looked happier and younger than she had for ages.

Davey chewed his bottom lip. Life was difficult. He couldn't be so selfish as to want Mum to be sad for ever, yet he wasn't happy about the way things were now. Was this what adults meant about turning back the clock? He certainly wished he could.

The errand was no chore. A winding path through a fringe of ragged trees led to the next cove and Sandybank Bakery, where Davey filled his lungs with the yummy smell of bread and cakes hot from the ovens.

Mrs Abercrombie greeted him with a warm smile. She knew him well from summers past.

"Hello, Davey. Usual order, is it?" Her eyes crinkled at the corners with kindly understanding.

"How's your mum? Tell her to call round and catch up on the gossip."

As she spoke she bustled about wrapping a cottage loaf in waxy paper, then reached over to a tray of currant buns and popped one in a paper bag.

"I won't even ask if you're hungry — boys always are. That'll keep you going till teatime."

And she brushed away Davey's thanks with a wave of her hand.

OUTSIDE, Davey was trying to decide whether to eat his bun at once or wait until he reached the cottage when all thoughts of food were banished by the roar of a motorbike. Then a shiny red Suzuki screeched to a halt by some boys hauling a dinghy up from the shore.

The leather-clad rider shut down the engine, asking directions, and one of the boys pointed over the cliff, while his companions gaped at the magnificent machine, envy etched on their faces.

It really was a beautiful bike. Dad would have loved it. But Davey knew he wouldn't mention it to Richard — he just wouldn't be interested.

Davey's mood lightened as he made his way back along the narrow cliff path, munching his spiced bun. He guessed it would be some time before Mum had tea ready — they were bound to wait for Stephanie.

As he reached the headland, squabbling gulls wheeled around his head, hoping for a tasty crumb, but they were disappointed.

The white-sailed yacht was far out at sea now, making good progress and reminding Davey of the sailing lessons Dad had promised him.

But, before he had time to grow down-hearted again, he noticed, on the cliff top where the lane petered out and the steps to the beach began, the red Suzuki he had seen earlier by Sandybank Bakery.

His eyes searched the beach for a sight of the rider. It was almost deserted — just one family left, collecting buckets and spades and packing towels into a beach bag. Late afternoon shadows darkened the cove. The sunbathing girls had long gone. Where could the bike rider be?

THEN, as he neared the holiday bungalow, Davey stood stock still in amazement. Sitting on the wooden veranda was a slim figure in black leather. The silver helmet had been removed and spiky red hair framed a small face covered in freckles.

"Hi! Are you Dave?" the girl called when she looked up and saw him.

"Yes!" he managed to croak, his mouth suddenly dry.

This couldn't be Stephanie, could it?

"Well, it's nice to meet you at last. I'm . . ."

"Stephanie!" he supplied, before she could finish.

"Oh, no, only my dad calls me that!" She laughed. "My friends call me Steph. You don't have the door key, do you, Dave? I'm dying of thirst after that journey."

They sat, either side of the kitchen table, drinking cola. Davey was speechless as he gazed at this girl, not much bigger than him, but so full of life and enthusiasm.

"This is a great place, isn't it?" She motioned around. "Swimming! Surfing! You'll have to show me round. The best beaches. Everything!"

"Yes. Sure." She wasn't anything like he'd expected. She certainly wasn't at all like Richard!

"I've always hated being an only child," she was saying. "I don't know about you, Dave, but I'm glad I've got a new brother."

He liked the way she called him "Dave". It made him feel as if they were the same age.

"Yes, I've always wanted a brother, too," he answered, caught off guard.

"And now you've got me. Never mind, I've always been a tomboy." She grinned again, then her expression changed and her bright blue eyes seemed to darken.

"We both know what it's like to lose someone special, Dave. I guess we have a lot in common really. I wasn't too happy when Dad told me about Carol, but now I've met you I feel lots better."

She turned away and gazed out of the window. Davey thought he knew why, too. She didn't want him to see the tears in her eyes. He hadn't realised it would be just as hard for Stephanie as it was for him.

"Now, where can I put this gear, Dave?" She was gathering leathers and helmet from the floor where they had been dropped. "Then we'll go and meet my dad and your mum — or shall we say Richard and Carol?"

"Yes!" His face split into a huge grin. "I'd like that a lot, Steph."

And, suddenly, Davey's summer and beyond looked a whole lot brighter. ■

Coming Home

By Marjorie Santer.

ALISON wandered over to the garden chair and sat down, resting her arms on the wrought iron table. She cupped her chin in one hand and with the other idly traced the table's intricate pattern.

"I'll take you with me," she said aloud. "Jenny would never forgive me if I left her birthday present behind."

She sighed, thinking of all the decisions ahead of her, but before her troubled thoughts could take further shape, a voice claimed her attention.

"Cooee! Are you there, Alison?"

"Oh, hi, Maggie. Come in, love. I'm up in the picnic place." She got up stiffly and walked down the winding path to meet her next-door neighbour.

"Coffee?"

"Oh, yes, please. I'd love one."

They strolled companionably down to the back door of the big old house and busied themselves in the kitchen. Picking up their cups, Alison urged her friend outside again.

"Let's sit outside. It's such a lovely day."

"Mmm. Amazing for this time of year. Look how bare the trees are."

"Oh, don't. It's a nightmare trying to clear all those leaves up."

Maggie put her head on one side and looked at her with a grin.

"Just think! It's not your nightmare any longer. Someone else will be doing all that clearing up. Now there's a happy thought!"

Alison sighed.

"Yes, you're right — and to tell you the truth I could do with some happy thoughts right now."

"Why, what's wrong? I thought you were so pleased with the idea of moving."

"Oh, yes, I am. But I shall miss this garden, Maggie. We built it up from scratch, Henry and I. Do you remember what it was like when we moved in all those years ago?"

"Don't I just! We all felt sorry for you, having to tackle such a wilderness."

"We felt sorry for ourselves at first and then we began to enjoy it. Not that Henry would know it now! I've altered so much.

"Bless his heart, he was a real worker, but never all that interested in planting flowers. He left that to me. The vegetable garden was his pride and joy."

Maggie sipped her coffee and nodded.

"I must say I miss all the green beans and apples that came over my fence!"

THEY left the picnic place and walked beyond to where Alison had converted the despised vegetable garden into a huge pond where a small shoal of goldfish were lazily enjoying the unusual winter sunshine and nudging at the abundant plants she had planted at the edges.

"The new owner-to-be is a very keen gardener apparently. He was over the moon about the garden when he and his wife first came to look round. So that's all right. I know it will all be looked after."

They walked on, stepping down into the herb garden. Alison ran her fingers through aromatic sprigs of rosemary.

"Just look at this, Maggie. It's got so neglected." Her voice was worried and she bent to tug at some weeds.

"Come along, love. Don't start weeding now. It won't come to any harm if it's left for a while."

"I suppose not. But what I must do, Maggie, is decide what I can take with me from the garden. The garden at the bungalow is only small but if I take some bits and pieces of my favourite plants it will make it

Illustration by Sally Rowe.

seem more like home. Henry's favourites were always the spring flowers." Her voice faltered.

"He . . . he loved the snowdrops. We always used to watch for the first ones to come up under that old apple tree."

"They were always a picture. I daresay if you dug deep enough you could find some to take with you."

"Maybe. I'll have to see."

Maggie left then, after arranging to come round later to help Alison with her sorting and packing, for her moving day was looming ever closer.

THE next few weeks were hectic but at last everything was packed and ready to go. Alison had even managed to pot up a few precious plants to take with her.

She was unlucky with the snowdrops because she had left looking for them until the last minute and then couldn't find the tiny bulbs buried deep beneath other plants. She decided to buy new ones later on.

On her last evening in her old home, she wandered into the garden and looked back across the wide lawn towards the big old house that held so many happy memories for her.

Memories of her children growing up, filling the place with noise and laughter . . . and a few tears.

She remembered the birthday parties with games of hide and seek which later gave way to more sophisticated barbecues.

On the day of Jenny's wedding they had squeezed a huge marquee on to the lawn and Henry had festooned the trees with fairy lights.

There was an ache at the back of her throat and she blinked away a tear and jumped up, scolding herself.

Alison Parker, she told herself, you're getting maudlin. That little bungalow is delightful and you know it. And the garden will soon be just how you want it.

She scrubbed at her eyes and, tilting her chin, marched back into the house to finish her last bits of packing.

* * * *

The time flew past and Alison was so busy that she really had no time to look back. Jenny was expecting her second baby in January so Alison went to stay with her for Christmas.

"I'm so glad you're here, Ma. I don't know how I would have coped with Christmas. I feel like a beached whale! And I get tired out so easily, doing the slightest thing!"

"Oh, you would have managed if you'd had to," Alison answered briskly. "All the same, I'm glad I'm here to help." She busily rolled out another batch of pastry.

The Romantic Couple

Arm-in-arm, and
heart-to-heart,
So gracefully they glide
Over the ice, Rebecca
and Rob,
Close to each other's
side;

She, with her bonnet
tied under her chin,
Bonny and blithe,
and neat as a
pin,
And he, with his
old-world, gentle charm,
So proud of the lassie on
his arm.

Oh, may they glide through the
years ahead,
Their joys and sorrows
to share,
And fate be kind to Rebecca and Rob,
Who make such a perfect pair;

Staying as close as they are today,
In love, in the sweet, old-fashioned way,
May this happy Yuletide be the start
Of a lifetime together — heart-to-heart!

— Kathleen O'Farrell.

She wasn't really looking forward to returning to the bungalow, but Jenny went into labour earlier than expected and so she stayed to hold the fort.

The new baby was a delightful little girl, bonnie and healthy, but there were complications for Jenny.

Alison stayed on for several weeks until all was well and her daughter was able to cope with everything.

"I don't know how we can thank you, Ma," Jenny said as she hugged her mother goodbye.

"I've enjoyed it, love. Every bit of it . . . and thank you for my new granddaughter. She's a treasure."

"Am I a treasure too, Grandma?" said a small voice by her knees, and she bent down to pick Paul up and hug him breathless.

"You're my best treasure," she assured him before getting into the car where Jake, her son-in-law, was waiting to take her home.

"Home," she thought as they sped along. "It won't feel like home."

The journey was short, for the new bungalow was much closer than her old home had been. That had been one of the bonuses.

"I won't stay," Jake said, as they arrived. "I want to get back for Jenny before it gets dark, so I'll just see you safely inside. Will that be all right? Will you be OK?"

"Of course, love. I shall be fine."

She waved him off and turned back into the house, thinking once again that it wouldn't feel like home.

BUT she was wrong. Her deep and comfortable armchairs with the chintzy covers that she and Henry had chosen together welcomed her like old friends. The old blue plates on her dresser reminded her, as always, of holidays in Holland — and the sonorous ticking of the grandfather clock, a much-prized wedding present from her long-gone parents, reminded her that all her home was still around her.

And, somehow, so was Henry.

She thought of all the time she had just spent with her family and of the love they had shared, and was content.

Dropping her coat on to a chair, she went into the kitchen to put the kettle on. As she filled it she gazed out of the window into the garden beyond . . . and was transfixed.

All around the edges of the tiny lawn, in all the flower-beds and under the tree in the corner, were snowdrops. Hundreds of snowdrops. Like a carpet of pearly white.

"Oh, Henry!" Alison said. "If only you could see this."

She laughed.

"I bet you knew about it all the time."

She was home. ■

THE trouble with Will is that he won't stop bringing me presents. Maybe it's his way of telling me he loves me. I get a little something nearly every day, and often it's of the disgusting variety.

Yesterday was a prime example.

"Oh, Will, that is gross," I'd screamed ungratefully, stepping over his latest offering.

Luckily, I'd just finished washing up and was still wearing my rubber gloves, so it was disposed of immediately. With a wrapping of newspaper, the latest in a long line of unwanted gifts was dropped deftly into the dustbin.

He'd brought me mice, birds, even a rabbit once. Will was so proud of his hunting skills.

A few of his little delicacies had been dragged as far as the kitchen. So far, only one had got further, and that was the worst. He'd managed to carry half a frog all the way up the stairs.

A whole frog wouldn't have been so bad, but half! And don't ask which half because I didn't look

Something The Cat Dragged In!

by Lynne Hackles.

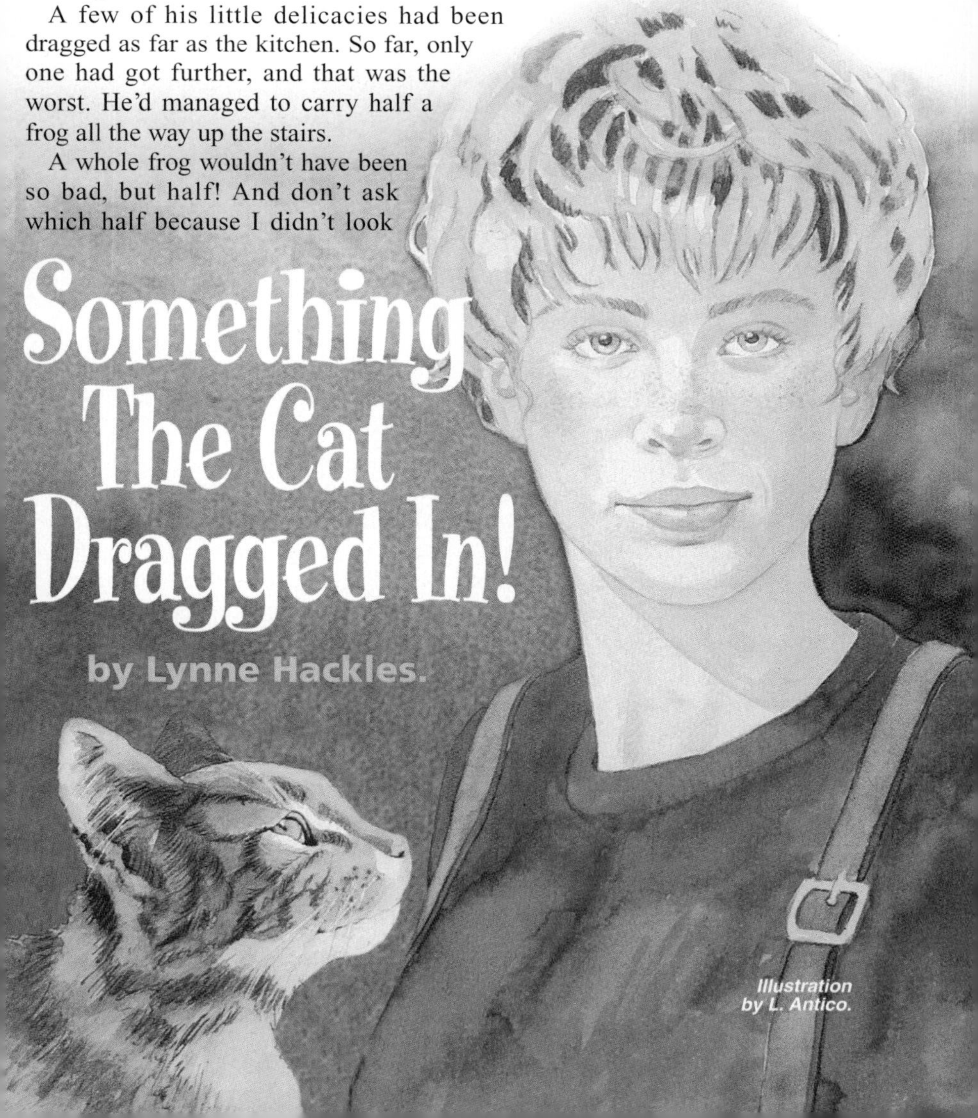

Illustration by L. Antico.

that closely. It was green with two legs and that's all anyone needs to know.

Begging him not to deliver any more bodies hadn't worked. According to a pet psychologist on the television, the trick was not to make a big thing of it. You should pick up the pressie and drop it without fuss into the bin. Once it was established that the gifts were unwelcome they'd stop.

Fat chance, I thought at the time, but there had been a change in Will's behaviour and, although the actual bearing of gifts continued, he was definitely getting more adventurous in his choices.

This morning's present was spectacularly different.

"What on earth have you brought me now?" I demanded, holding the offending item aloft, between finger and thumb.

Can a cat look amused? I'd swear old Will had a smirk on his whiskered face. He stared up at me and nonchalantly began washing a paw.

Then there was a knock at the door.

"Hellooo," Deirdre called. That's what she always does. Calls and then walks straight in.

Today, I panicked. My mouth dropped open, and I did a nervous little jig around the living-room, hoping that Will's latest offering would disappear. Needless to say, it didn't but, just as Deirdre appeared in the doorway, I had the sense to shove it behind a cushion.

"Are you all right?" she asked. "You look a bit flushed."

"Oh, I've been rushing," I lied.

My jaw dropped again as Deirdre settled herself in the very armchair and against the very cushion that Will's treasure was buried beneath.

DEIRDRE'S a treasure herself really. Since I moved here two months ago, she's taken on the position of honorary mother. She keeps an eye on me, gets my washing in if it rains while I'm at work, takes in parcels, waters my plants and feeds the cat if I'm away for the weekend.

It's great having her next door, having someone I can rely on, even if she does tend to be a little nosy on occasions.

"How's the love life?" she asked bluntly. Deirdre never beats about the bush.

"Non-existent." It was an honest answer, and I almost felt sorry that I didn't have some romantic news to impart when I saw the look on her face.

"I can't understand it," Deirdre said. "A nice girl like you should have them queuing up."

"I wish!" I laughed and went to put the kettle on.

Deirdre followed me into the kitchen, opened the cupboard and got out the biscuit tin.

Will wrapped himself around her legs. He always knows which of my friends aren't too fond of cats, and Deirdre fell into that category. She puts up with him but she's not a cat-person.

Prior to putting Will outside, I scooped him up into my arms and gave him a big kiss right between his ears and whiskers. He swished his tail but it made him purr like crazy.

"You spoil that cat," Deirdre said. "You should be lavishing your affection on a young man, not an animal. A girl of your age should be settled down. Are you sure there isn't someone?"

I dropped a tea bag into each mug and bit my tongue. Outside Will set up a loud wailing. Through the window we could see him sitting on top of the fence, eyeballing us.

"His full name was Pussy Willow," I told Deirdre, in an effort to change the subject, "but once I heard what he was capable of, it got changed to Weeping Willow."

"Suits him," Deirdre said, with a grim smile.

We took our drinks back into the living-room and settled ourselves for what, I hoped, would be a short chat.

It was actually shorter than I envisaged.

DEIRDRE fidgeted on the armchair, put her mug on the coffee table and began to rearrange the cushions. That was when she found Will's gift.

"What on earth are these?" she squealed, holding the offending item aloft, between finger and thumb. She sounded just like my mother.

I shrugged my shoulders and stared at the ceiling.

"And, more to the point, who do they belong to?"

What could I say? There was no answer to that one. To be honest, what she was waving left me pretty speechless.

Will, who must have re-entered via his cat-flap, sidled past, rubbing his back against my legs, asking for approval. He was smirking again.

"What are they?" Deirdre asked.

That was obvious.

"Purple nylon Y-fronts," I said.

"And who do they belong to?" she repeated. Her disapproving voice had reached glass-cracking proportions.

I thought it was a daft question. She must have known they weren't mine.

"Willow," I said.

Deirdre was very upset. She left in a hurry.

"I'll speak to you later," she warned over her shoulder, making her sound more like a mum than ever.

I felt awful. Was she annoyed with me because she thought I had a boyfriend and was keeping him hidden? Or, worse still, had I let her down by hiding his underwear? Either way, she must have thought I'd lied to her — and I would never do that.

"It's all your fault." I glared at Will. "Why do you have the loudest wail in history and a severe case of kleptomania?"

He looked up at me, winding himself around my ankles, asking for a kiss and cuddle which he didn't deserve. Next, he tried jumping on to my lap — difficult for us both, as I was standing. I sat down, let him get comfortable and began stroking his warm fur.

"Why can't you be a normal cat and why can't you'd stop bringing me presents?"

Will tilted his head to one side and wailed. He showed not the slightest remorse, so I pushed him away, stood up, brushed a few hairs from my black skirt and went to fetch my rubber gloves and a freezer bag in which to deposit the brightly-coloured underwear of an unknown person of the opposite sex.

I spent the remainder of the day wondering how to pacify Deirdre and decided that only the truth would do. But what was the truth? Some answers were needed.

* * * *

After a bowl of chicken and tuna, Will went for a stroll. It was time for me to turn detective. I picked up my parcel and followed him.

In the fading light we made our way along the lane which ran behind the houses. A dozen doors down, Will leaped nimbly over the fence.

I peered over the top and saw a line almost filled with large items of washing. In the centre was a gap. I sneaked in through the gate, picked up a peg from the path and stretched across to pin the purple pants in their proper place.

Of course, Will had to choose precisely that moment to serenade a slimline tabby sitting by the door.

Will serenades loudly and, before I knew what was happening we were all in the limelight. Spotlight, actually. Security spotlight.

"Gotcha!" a loud voice cried.

Will and the new girlfriend disappeared into the dusk, leaving me to face the music.

"I was putting them back," I assured the owner of the voice, praying at the same time that his was a man-eating patio which would hurry up and swallow me. "My cat stole them."

"I know. I spent half the morning chasing those undies and that furry thief." His voice was warm and friendly.

"You'd better come in and explain it all to my dad. They're his favourite pair," he confided. "Definitely not mine."

But I'd already deduced that.

"Then, would you return the favour and explain to my honorary mum?" I smiled at him, and at the thought of Deirdre meeting him. I was sure she was going to approve. ■

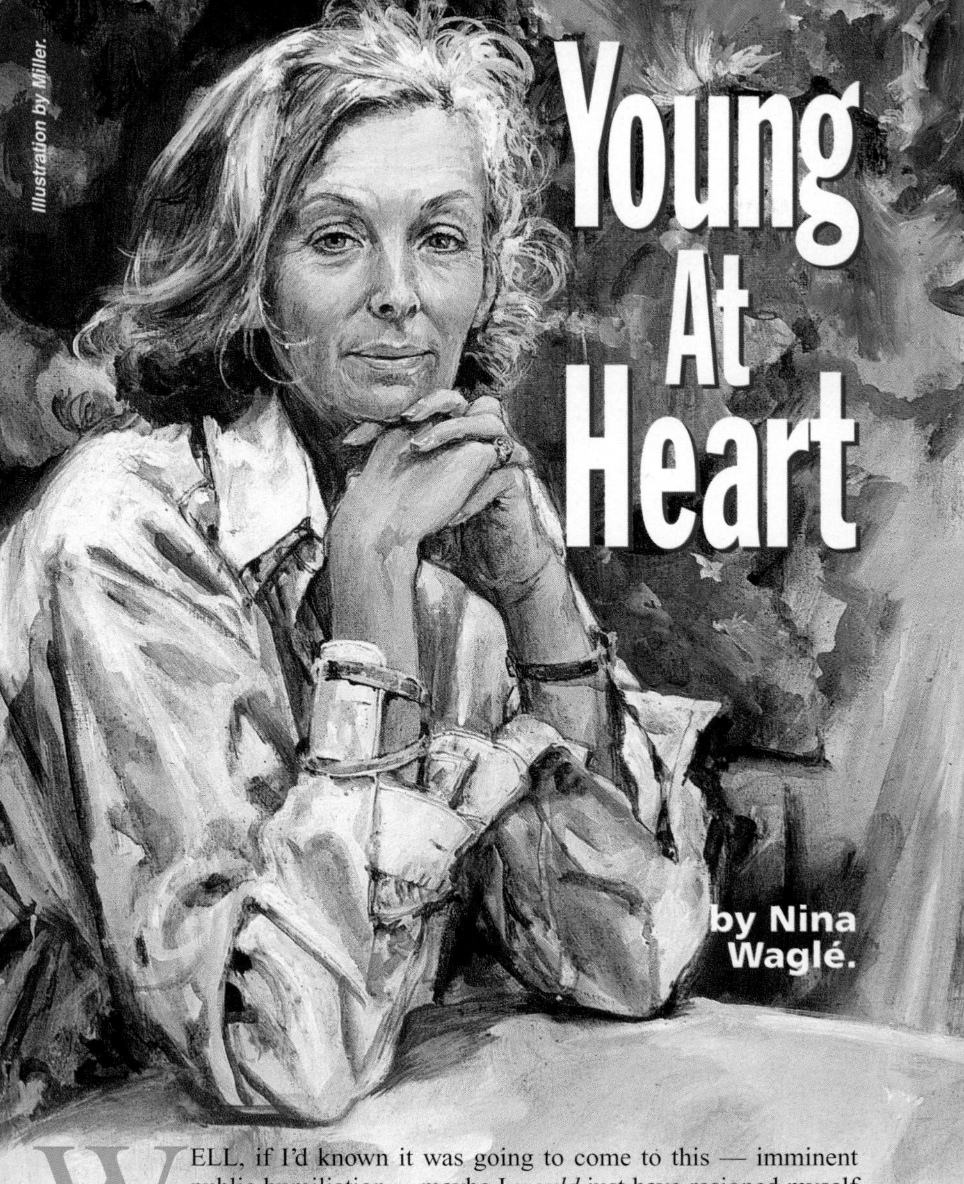

Young At Heart

by Nina Waglé.

WELL, if I'd known it was going to come to this — imminent public humiliation —maybe I *would* just have resigned myself to old age, as all my family seemed to think I would do. No, not only would do, but *should* do.

It all started a few months ago when my first grandchild was born. Now, don't get me wrong. Baby Jack is (in my unbiased opinion) the most beautiful baby in the world and I would fight any other grandmother tooth and nail if she tried to dispute it.

So I was, and still am, overjoyed, besotted, starry-eyed — well, you get the picture.

But I really do not see why, just because I am now a grandmother, I should suddenly change my whole personality. Being a grandmother does not make me old.

Because I am not old. Well, OK, I'm sixty-two, but that's nothing these days. And anyway, like my Len used to say, age is irrelevant. You are as old as you feel — it's all down to attitude.

Though, as I said, my family seem to have different ideas. A couple of weeks ago, Ella asked me what I wanted Jack to call me.

"What do you think, Mum? Nana or Grandma or Gran?"

Whilst I was pondering my answer, Steve, Ella's husband, chipped in.

"I guess you'll be thinking of slowing down a bit now, Jean. Now that you are a grandmother," he clarified.

I gave him what I hoped was a withering look.

"Why would I want to do that?"

"Well, my dad was just saying the other day that he hoped you understood the importance of your role in little Jack's life."

I drew myself up to my full five feet four.

"You can let Ian know that I understand the importance of my role perfectly well. I just hope that he does, too."

YOU see, it's been six years since I lost my Len, and Steve's mum, Doreen, died a couple of years ago. So little Jack was only going to have one grandmother and one grandfather.

And from Ian's point of view I just wasn't going to cut the mustard. Doreen, bless her, was a lovely lady, sweet and gentle, and, naturally enough, from Ian's point of view Doreen would have made the perfect grandmother — she enjoyed baking, knitting, gardening and she was a comfortable, cosy person.

I have to admit that I have always bought cakes from the bakers, I wouldn't know one end of a knitting needle from the other and let's just say I really do not have green fingers.

But none of that meant that I wouldn't be a perfectly good grandmother. As I informed Ian myself at Jack's christening.

Unfortunately, Ian and I, as family, had to share a pew. And the disapproving clicking noise he made when he saw me would have been enough to put anyone's teeth on edge.

"Is anything the matter?" I asked in a whisper.

He shook his head sorrowfully.

"I wouldn't have said anything," he muttered self-righteously, "but don't you think that outfit is a bit unsuitable?"

"Unsuitable?" I spluttered. From a man dressed in suit trousers that could well have dated from biblical days topped by a very questionable tweed jacket, this was a bit rich.

"Well, it's rather bright," he said lugubriously.

"It's a christening, Ian, not a funeral," I hissed back.

(Just so you know, I was wearing a perfectly elegant lime green trouser suit with a lovely matching hat.)

"But you've got to look ahead, Jean. Remember, young Jack won't want a grandmother who embarrasses him in public by dressing like a woman half her age."

For just a second I was speechless. Then I recovered.

"How dare you!" I screeched, forgetting to keep my voice low. "What Jack will want is a grandmother who loves him and is fun!" I paused for breath, ignoring the amused glances I was attracting.

"He'll need at least one of his grandparents to know the meaning of the word fun. And it obviously won't be you."

After that interchange, relations between Ian and myself were less than cordial.

And it seemed to me that whenever I was around at Ella's he was there, tickling Baby Jack, who'd gurgle with laughter, and glaring at me from under his bushy eyebrows with his irritatingly piercing blue eyes. And the more he glared at me the more outrageous I felt like being.

WHICH is why I blame Ian for the mess I am in now. If he hadn't been so scathing at the idea of me having a date I would never have agreed to have dinner with Eric and then I would never have been tempted to . . . well, anyway, let me tell this properly.

Eric belongs to the bridge club and, after Len died, it was Eric who eventually persuaded me to return to playing bridge again. I'll always be grateful to him for that, because I enjoy the social side just as much the game.

In fact, I no longer enjoy the game quite as much as before. I mean, don't get me wrong, Eric is actually a much better bridge player than Len was, but he does take winning very seriously.

When Len and I played, we didn't really mind whether we won or lost, although we tried our best, naturally. But somehow, with Eric, I do feel under more pressure to beat our opponents.

Eric and I were just bridge partners and good friends — nothing more. To be honest, he has always been a bit of a Casanova — he's still in his fifties, or so he claims, distinguished-looking, greying at the temples (though I suspect discreet use of hair dye myself), divorced and suave. His many conquests are the talk of the bridge club, where he has broken more than a few middle-aged hearts.

Eric always saw me as a bit of a challenge, I think, so every so often he asked me out for dinner and I always jokingly told him I was too old to be taken in by his charm.

So a few weeks ago I was telling Ella and Steve how Eric had asked me out again when Ian chipped in from the corner.

"Ridiculous," he muttered. I was beginning to wonder whether he had moved in permanently.

"What's ridiculous?" I snapped. "What is ridiculous about Eric asking me out?"

"People would talk. And he's younger than you for a start."

"Well, now you come to mention it, I've always fancied the idea of a toy boy," I flashed back.

"Thank you for that, Ian. You've made my mind up. I'll do it."

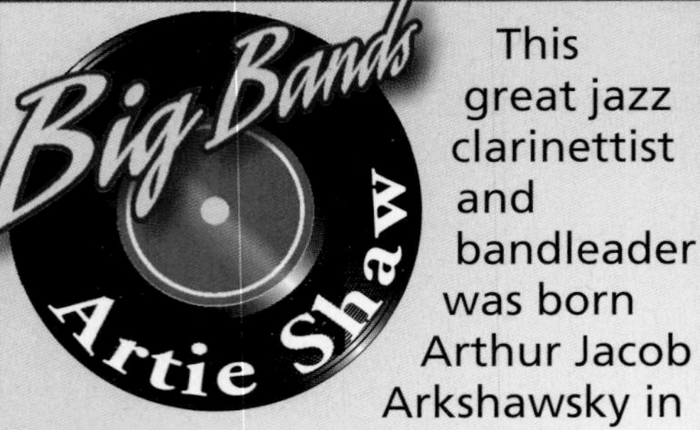

This great jazz clarinettist and bandleader was born Arthur Jacob Arkshawsky in 1910.

He had a hit with "Begin The Beguine" in 1937, and then, three years later, "Frenesi" topped the charts for twenty-three weeks!

Like his fellow bandleader, Benny Goodman, Artie Shaw employed black artists such as Billie Holliday at a time when this was not a common or popular practice.

Artie Shaw retired in the 1960s, and eventually became a writer and novelist.

SO I went out for dinner with Eric. And very pleasant it was, too. He wined me and dined me, complimented my appearance, discussed the latest films and it ended up with me agreeing to another date. And another, despite the running commentary from Ian.

Which, I suppose, is why I agreed to the dance marathon . . . I could just picture Ian's horror when he heard that Eric and I had entered an over-Fifties charity dance marathon.

I have to admit that I maybe exaggerated my level of fitness and my dancing ability to Eric *slightly* but I was sure it didn't matter — it wasn't the Olympics or anything.

To be honest, I was really looking forward to it. I have always loved dancing and I was a bit of a dab hand at it in my day.

I twirled Baby Jack around and told him all about it, how Grandpa Len and Granny Jean had danced in their courting days.

Then I told him all about Len, and how much Len would have loved his grandson, and how I knew, just knew that Len was watching over him.

Pictorial Press.

I suppose I got a bit carried away until I heard the gruff noise of a throat clearing. It was Ian.

I turned to wipe my eyes surreptitiously before facing him. To my surprise he had a smile on his face.

"I do that, too," he said quietly. "Tell Jack about his other gran. I know Doreen would have loved him."

Just as I was feeling a slight sense of warming to him, the smile disappeared as quickly as it had arrived.

"Listen, Jean." The eyebrows descended into their familiar bushy frown. "About this dance marathon. I think . . ."

"I'm too old for that sort of thing. That a sensible grandmother wouldn't be doing anything that could be classed as fun," I finished for him, my temper rising.

"Well, it may surprise you to hear that I am not remotely interested in what you think I should do. I *know* what you think I should do, Ian. Stay at home and knit and bake. Well, I'm not Doreen."

I stopped, horrified with myself. I had had no right to say that. But I suppose secretly I was worried that Ian was right — that I wasn't as good a grandmother as Doreen would have been.

"I'm sorry," I said, and withdrew with as much dignity as I could.

THAT was a week ago and I haven't heard from Ian since. He hasn't even been at Ella's when I've gone round to see Jack.

But at the moment I have more to worry about. I arrived at the dance marathon looking my best, I have to say. I splashed out on a beautiful dress just like the ones I wore back in my younger days and I must admit I think I look pretty good.

There were a lot of people I know there and I noticed that everyone was giving me slightly odd looks.

Suddenly I heard Ian's voice in my head.

"Dressed like a woman half your age."

Doubts started to creep in. Where was Eric? Surely he hadn't let me down? Suddenly I saw him heading towards me and I breathed a sigh of relief.

Until I saw the woman walking next to him. If she was over fifty I would eat my whole collection of hats.

Eric smiled at me.

"Jean, I am so sorry. I really have been meaning to call. The thing is, I've found a new partner. I enjoyed dancing with you — it's just that I think I've got more of a chance of winning with Lisa. I know you'll understand. Wish us luck!"

And he sauntered away, seemingly oblivious to my distress and embarrassment. Leaving me standing here in all my finery. Publicly humiliated.

I could see the sideways glances. The pitying looks and the shaking heads. The whispered comments.

"Another one of Eric's broken-hearted ladies."

HOW could I have been so stupid? When did Eric ever enter anything for fun? It was all about winning to him — and if he had found a younger, fitter partner than a sixty-two-year-old grandmother, he would have seen nothing wrong in going off with her. It was just the way he was — and I shouldn't have been surprised when it happened. But knowing all this didn't make me feel any better.

Suddenly, the thought of being a nice, cosy granny safely tucked up in a tartan rug in a rocking-chair, knitting needles in hand, becomes amazingly appealing.

And then, out of nowhere, I see that there is a man coming towards me. A man with bushy eyebrows and piercing blue eyes, dressed to kill in a tuxedo that looks remarkably like the ones they used to wear forty years ago.

He smiles tentatively at me.

"Need a partner?" he asks diffidently. "I used to be a bit of Fred Astaire in my younger days."

And my heart, my sixty-two-year-old heart, gives a little leap as I step towards him. He takes my hands and before I know it we are whirling round the floor as if we had been practising together for months. We are so comfortable with each other. So in tune. I can hardly believe this is the same man.

"It's a shame Baby Jack can't see his grandparents now," I say as he twirls me expertly round.

"There'll be plenty of time for that," Ian says, a gleam of fun in his eyes.

And somehow I know there will be. ■

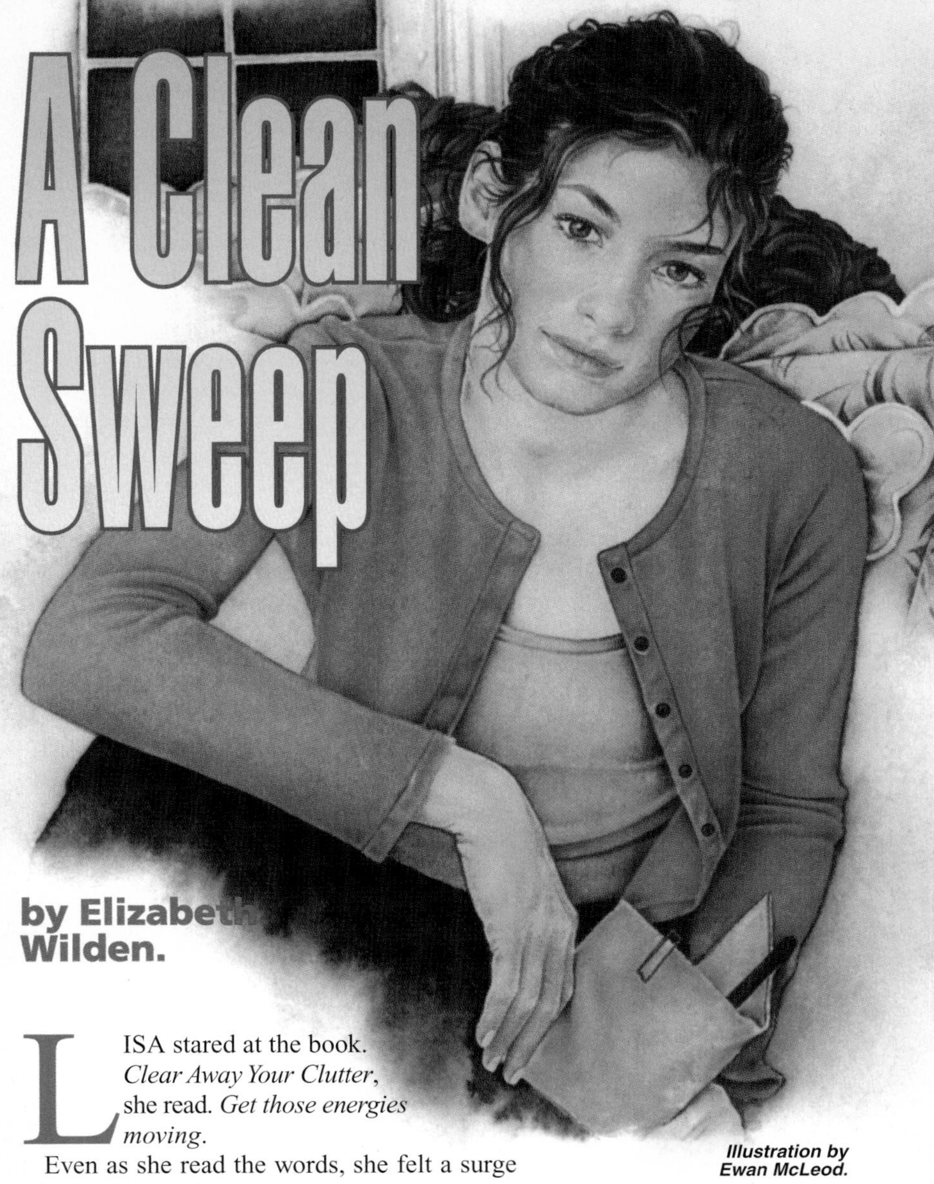

A Clean Sweep

by Elizabeth Wilden.

Illustration by Ewan McLeod.

LISA stared at the book. *Clear Away Your Clutter*, she read. *Get those energies moving*.

Even as she read the words, she felt a surge of energy move through her. It was anger.

Rob was always telling her how untidy she was.

"I thought it might motivate you into cleaning up this mess," he said. "How can you live like this?"

His eyes roved around the room and his nose wrinkled in disgust.

Lisa clenched her fists and tried to smile.

"Thanks," she mumbled.

She'd promised to have a bit of a tidy-up but hadn't got round to it.
"It's difficult knowing what to get rid of and what to keep," she told him.
"That's why I bought you the book," Rob said, a trifle smugly. "We don't want you turning into a slob, do we?"
When she was alone that evening, she picked up the book, thinking that any help was welcome. She hated to admit it, but Rob was right. The place *was* a tip.
Over the past six months, since she'd met Rob, everything seemed to have multiplied. Cupboards, drawers, even whole rooms were overflowing.
"Chuck it all out," Rob had said.
Lisa knew that, if he had his way, all her prized belongings would go to the tip, and she would find herself in a replica of his flat.
What did he call it? Minimalist. Empty, more like. He had a few pieces of furniture, three matching candles and a peace lily in a glass tube.
She skipped the section on Feng Shui. There simply wasn't room to rearrange her furniture. What she needed was some advice on what to do and how to do it.
"Ah, this is it," she said, smoothing the pages open at the chapter headed *Getting Rid*. But it was nothing to do with telling you what to keep and what to get rid of. It was all to do with being stuck in a rut and not being able to move forward because you were hanging on to the past by keeping hold of possessions.

LISA flicked over another couple of pages and found a quiz. It was the sort she always enjoyed in magazines.
Are you a hoarder? it asked. *Is your spare room, A: ready for guests, or B: used for storage?*
That was easy. Rob had suggested she clear her wardrobe a few days previously and all the clothes she couldn't make decisions about were piled on the spare bed.
In one corner was stacked a pile of useful items such as the clock radio and the slow cooker she never used. There was nowhere else to put them.
Definitely B.
Do your kitchen cupboards hold, A: any out of date items, or B: only foodstuffs in regular use?
Lisa thought of the old Christmas pudding and the packet of cracked wheat she'd never thrown out and didn't know what to do with. That was A then.
As she made her way through the questions she got a distinct feeling that she wasn't doing very well, so the high score she accumulated came as no surprise. She turned to the back of the book to see what it said about fifty-six points.
How can you breathe? it screamed at her. *Your space is well and truly cluttered. You are going to have to get tough. Drastic action is called for.*

Refer to the Five Pile Plan on page 22 as soon as possible.

Lisa stifled a yawn.

"Too tired to get tough tonight," she told the book. 'I'm off to bed. Tomorrow's going to be a busy day."

AND it was. Lisa became more and more brutal as she tackled each room. The old Christmas pudding, the cracked wheat and a whole lot of other stuff she didn't know she owned went on to Pile One. Junk. Things she could live without.

The bin bag for Pile Two was stuffed with paperbacks and topped with fashion blunders in assorted sizes ready to go to a charity shop.

Pile Three, repairs or alterations, became an extension of the junk heap. Lisa knew she'd never get round to putting a new zip in the old jeans or super-gluing heads on ornaments.

Switching on the kettle, she came to a decision. The clock radio and the slow cooker she could live without. That got rid of Pile Four, things she wanted to keep but needed to find somewhere to keep them.

Pile Five was the dither heap. Shall I keep? Shan't I keep? According to the rules, six months was allowed before making up your mind. If you hadn't used the item or items in question within that time then you didn't need them at all.

Lisa took her coffee and flopped into the armchair. It was Rob who'd told her she lived in a mess and she'd begun to believe him, but this exercise had been an eye-opener. She wasn't such a hoarder after all.

She sipped at her drink. It had worked. Her flat felt clearer, cleaner, emptier. Her head felt clearer, too. And she felt so good about herself for making all those decisions about what to keep and what to let go of. It was easy once you got going. Perhaps that was what was meant by *getting the energies moving*?

Lisa stood up. There was one last thing to do — dispose of Pile Six.

The book hadn't mentioned this one. It was the pile the world's leading expert in clutter-clearing knew nothing about. Lisa had discovered it all by herself.

* * * *

Half an hour later, she let herself into Rob's flat and scattered a little of Pile Six into each of his rooms.

Rob's trainers. Rob's jacket. Rob's books, CDs, sports kit, half his wardrobe, pens and diaries, old magazines and newspapers.

His place was transformed.

Lisa smiled as she carefully placed the "Clear Away Your Clutter" book between Rob's three matching candles and his peace lily.

She hoped he would get the message. ■

Letters From The Past

by A.J. Redcliffe.

DO you mind very much if I ask you a question? What would you do if you came across a letter, in an envelope, addressed to someone else, and the envelope was open? Would you — you know what I'm going to say — would you read it?

Well, of course you wouldn't, I know.

But what if it was obviously a very old letter? What if you could actually see the date of the postmark? Would you read it then? I'm asking because it happened to me.

In my retirement I moved from England to Ireland, where I had cousins and had spent holidays with many happy memories. And so I bought a cottage, a bit rundown but pretty, just outside Clifden in County Galway.

Everybody leaves their mark on where they live. Sometimes it's almost as tangible as a footprint in wet cement, sometimes just a feeling, an atmosphere. My cottage had an atmosphere that I liked as soon as I set foot in it. It felt like coming home.

All I needed to do was decorate and furnish it to my taste and throw out any rubbish, any remnants of the past. That was when I found the letter.

Well, I must be honest, there was a small bundle of three letters.

It was one rainy day, a few weeks after moving in. I was sorting out some odds and ends, long-abandoned bits and pieces, in an old box in the outhouse in the kitchen garden.

I certainly wasn't sifting through the contents of the box, and I'll blame what happened next on fate, or at least on the mouse.

I'd picked up a bundle of yellowing old newspapers and was about to drop

Illustration by David Axtell.

them into a black bin-liner when the little creature scuttled over my foot. I dropped my bundle in surprise.

I bent to pick up the scattered papers, smiling at the thought that I had been the "cow'rin, tim'rous beastie" this time. Then I saw the little package of letters that had been hidden in among the newspapers.

They lay on the floor, a pathetic little bundle, tied with a cross of rough string. No pink ribbon with a bow, no fading perfume. They didn't look romantic or exciting, but as I was soon to discover, they told a story — a love story.

Even before I picked them up, I could see that they were old. The handwriting was careful copperplate, thin lines but bold and clear, the product of a steel nib dipped into black ink, scratching over cheap, rough paper.

They were certainly old letters. And that was why I opened the first one.

I stood in that gloomy little outhouse in the year 2004, with the gentle autumn rain pattering down, bringing the fresh scent of the grass, and I stepped back in time, over a hundred years, into the lives of two strangers, two lovers . . .

To Miss N. Muldoon, Ross Cottage, Clifden.

My Dear Niamh,

I have arrived well enough in Liverpool and found lodging. It is a poor, rough place but with some decent families. I will not be here long, at least. I think of you, Niamh.

All the talk here is of the great things in America. There are fortunes to be made, they say. I don't need a fortune, Niamh, just enough for us.

And now for the great news! The next letter you have from me, my dear girl, will be from the United States itself, for I sail on the ninth for Boston! My ticket has nearly cleaned me out, but I know I will soon find work and I'll be working for us.

I give my best wishes now to your ma and da, and I give my heart to you, Niamh. How I love to write that sweet name!

God bless you.

Patrick Regan.

As I finished the letter and looked out at the tippling rain, I wondered how many more letters like this had been written by hopeful young men to anxious young girls, before Ireland's history had become America's history, or Canada's, or Australia's.

I wondered if Patrick had made his fortune and sent for his Niamh. I wondered if Niamh, perhaps sitting in the very garden I looked out on, had read and re-read her letter from Patrick and waited for the next one, for news from far across the sea.

I pulled up an old chair and sat and unfolded the second letter.

It was on different paper, but still cheap, and still in the same hand, thin but strong. I could see Niamh opening it full of expectation, hope, worry.

My Dearest Niamh,

How sorry I was to hear the sad news of your mother. At least, my dearest, there was no pain, no suffering, except of course, my dear girl, your own pain.

I know you will be feeling low. My thoughts and my prayers are with you every day.

As I told you, Boston was a grand place but there were more Irish there than Liverpool, and no jobs. But I was lucky, as I said, to fall in with John Duffy on his way to join his brother in Canada.

John spoke for me, the good man that he is, and I've got work.

Niamh, I'm building a railway! It's called the Canadian Pacific Railway, across the whole of Canada, Niamh — thousands of miles, and work for years. Perhaps I can send for you soon, my love. I read and re-read your letters.

Please give my deepest sympathy to your father.

God bless you always.

Patrick.

The Policeman

Up and down the street he goes,
And all around the Square,
Peter the peeler, on his beat,
With his stern, official air,
Keeping the peace, and
making sure
People, and property,
are secure.

But everywhere seems
calm today,
Good will and quiet
prevail,
No pickpockets to
apprehend,
Or naughty boys
to nail.
But wait — there's
Ragamuffin Joe,
Holding a snowball,
poised to throw!

I hope that isn't meant for me,
Thinks Pete, puffed up
with dignity.
For, if it were, a deed so dark
Might just be brushed off,
as a lark,
And Peter never would catch Joe,
Who'd leg it home — like Billy-o!

— Kathleen O'Farrell.

So Patrick was doing well, but Niamh had lost her mother. There was one letter left. What did that contain?

The rain was heavier, the sky darker. Was it an omen for Niamh and her Patrick?

The envelope of the third letter was in the same hand, but the quality of the paper was better. It was neatly addressed, in a bolder hand. As I carefully unfolded the single sheet and began to read, I thought the tone matched the lowering sky.

Dear Niamh,

I cannot believe what you say. Now is the time, Niamh, now is the time! Why are you hesitating?

It may be difficult for you to appreciate, but I'm a man of some importance here. The railway is going through the most beautiful and savage country and I direct hundreds of men, many of them hard-working Chinese fellows.

Your father is dear to you, I know, but you can't tie yourself to him. You've done your duty, Niamh. Your future must be with me.

I am still boarding with John Duffy and now his sister, Kathleen, has recently arrived. She's a pleasant, sweet young woman, and you would like her, I know.

Niamh, let me send you the tickets. You must choose, my dearest, and choose me — us, together in Canada. I love you, Niamh, and will never let you go.

Yours truly,

Patrick.

THREE miles from Dundee city centre lies Den o' Mains, scene from 1976 to 1985 of a major rescue operation. Mains Castle was originally built by Sir David Graham for himself and his bride, Dame Margaret Ogilvy, of the Airlie family, in the sixteen hundreds.

The Latin inscription above a doorway means "grateful for country, friends and posterity".

The castle fell on hard times, however, and in 1913 was bought from the Erskine family by the local council to form part of Caird Park, donated to the city by Sir James Caird for recreation. Now devotedly refurbished, Mains Castle boasts a splendid restaurant and remains one of Dundee's most photographed buildings.

The rain had stopped. I looked out at the dripping garden where, perhaps, Niamh had sat to read her letter from a distant land, from a man she had not seen in four years.

And perhaps in the house at that time sat another man, by a turf fire, his mind on the past, while in the garden his daughter's mind was on the future, her heart and her mind torn apart.

Had there been a tiny spasm of fear in Niamh's heart at the name of Kathleen? What had she done? What did Patrick do? Anything? Nothing?

There were no more letters. I looked, but there was nothing. Sunlight slanted through the doorway as I looked up and out, up to the hill above the village, where the wet spire of the church caught the sun.

There was one way of finding an ending to their story. There wasn't much chance of success, but I had to try.

WELL, there I was, like a fool on a fool's errand, in the middle of a country churchyard, not even sure what I was searching for.

I looked at this corner and that row, but soon became lost in a maze of Celtic crosses, carved blank-eyed angels and stone-weathered Madonnas.

In places the grass was knee high and wet. On many stones, inscriptions were barely visible, green and old and worn.

And then a name caught my eye, and my heart sank.

From a slanting stone it jumped out at me — *Niamh Muldoon*. I walked over to it. Was the love story over?

Niamh Muldoon fell asleep in the Lord, October 7, 1891.

But the date was wrong! This couldn't be my Niamh. Of course, this was her mother. It was Niamh's mother!

There was more beneath that.

Joseph Muldoon died May 4, 1901.

No more names, but as I turned away, like a little miracle it stood before me — a newer, lighter gravestone with the name I had been looking for.

Patrick Regan died June 20, 1952. Niamh, his wife, died March 1, 1954.

I bent and rubbed away the yellow-green lichen to trace the words with my finger. So Patrick had come back to her. He'd left Canada, and Kathleen, and the Canadian Pacific Railway, and come back to Ireland, to Clifden and to Niamh. Just when he did, I don't know and never will.

I left the lovers in peace, my heart feeling lighter and the mystery solved. Walking down from the top of the hill to the Muldoons' cottage, in the distance I caught a glimmer of the setting evening sun on the vast Atlantic ocean.

How did I know it was my Patrick and my Niamh? In the bottom corner of that stone, a maple leaf and a shamrock had been carved, intertwined. The story hadn't ended the way I thought, but it had ended happily enough. ■

Line Dancing For Beginners

by Rob Brown.

"I'M far too old for this!" Angela muttered. "Why did I ever let Mhairi talk me into it?"

She peered gloomily into the mirror on the wall, thinking resignedly of the time when mirrors told her a different story — when she was slim and lithe and could wear any of the latest fashions. These days, she was much happier leaving all that to Mhairi.

The doorbell rang once, and she heard the sound

Illustration by Gerard Fay.

of Mhairi's key in the lock. Her daughter bounced into the room with all the vitality of youth.

"Hi, Mum!" she said cheerily. "You look great!"

"I don't feel it!" Angela grumbled.

Mhairi grinned.

"It's about time you got out and about again," she said. "You're still a young woman."

Angela raised her eyebrows.

"Well — comparatively!"

A worried look crossed Angela's face.

"You know, I don't think I'll go after all. I know I'll just feel so out of place."

Mhairi patted her hand.

"Don't be silly!" she said. "You'll be fine. And Ben will be picking us up in a few minutes."

Good old Ben, Angela thought. He'd been so kind to her — always offering to drive her around in his taxi, always cheerful, even on her dark days.

Ben had been one of Lewis's oldest friends. They were so alike at times, she thought — and at others so completely different. They had been good friends long before Angela had come on the scene, but luckily she and Ben had always got on well.

She sighed.

Now, if only he were coming with them, she might feel more comfortable. Of all things — line dancing!

YOU'LL enjoy it when you get there, Mum!" Mhairi said enthusiastically.

"I really don't know why I ever agreed . . ." Angela sat down suddenly on a chair.

"Oh, Mum! Come on! It's not anything to get upset about." Mhairi sat down beside her and put a comforting arm round her shoulders.

"Dad wouldn't have wanted you to stay in and be miserable," she said quietly.

Angela nodded. Lewis would have encouraged her. She could just hear his voice saying, "You don't know until you try, Ange! Go for it!"

The beginnings of a smile lifted the corners of her mouth.

"That's more like it!" Mhairi said.

"There's just one thing, though," Angela said darkly. "I'm not going to wear a hat!"

Ben was waiting for them at the front gate at the appointed time. When he saw the stetson in Mhairi's hand, he grinned.

"That is a mighty fine hat, Ah do declare!"

"That's enough of that, Ben!" Mhairi said sharply. "Mum's nervous enough as it is!"

Ben smiled at Angela.

"Nervous?" he said. "Why?"

"I've never done anything like this before!" she said. She glanced at him hopefully.

"Why don't you come along and keep me company?"

Ben shook his head emphatically.

"Oh, no! Sorry, Angela — it's not my scene! Driving I do. Dancing, I don't! Got two left feet when it comes to dancing!"

They drove in silence for a few minutes.

"Tell me," Ben said at last, "because I'd really like to know. Do you wear the hat or is it for dancing round? You know, instead of the traditional handbag?"

"Certainly not," Mhairi retorted defensively, while Angela smothered a giggle. "You dance in a line — that's why it's called line dancing!"

"Oh. Sounds like great fun."

"It is! It's a super way to keep fit and meet people. Mum's going to have the time of her life!" Mhairi squeezed her mother's hand.

THE car slowed to a stop outside the Jubilee Hall.

"Here we are, pardners!" Ben announced. "Y'all have a great time!"

Angela reluctantly got out of the car.

"Thanks for the lift — again," she said.

"You sure are welcome, ma'am!" He looked up at her, straight into her eyes, and something she saw there sent a totally unexpected tingle down her spine. She was so surprised she almost gasped.

The next moment, Mhairi had grabbed her arm and was hurrying her inside.

"Come on, Mum. We don't want to miss the start!"

Recovering, Angela looked around the hall. There were about twenty people altogether — mostly women, but a few men as well. All wore leather boots and jeans; some of the men had checked shirts and cowboy hats. To Angela, the whole thing looked faintly ridiculous.

"This is Carol," Mhairi said, as a lady approached them. "She runs the group."

"Hello!" Carol said brightly, and they shook hands. "Always pleased to welcome new members."

"Oh — I'm not a new member," Angela said quickly. "I'm just here to see if I like it."

"You will, you will!" everyone chorused, but Angela wasn't so sure.

Carol and Mhairi introduced her to the rest of the group. Most of them wore the universal garb of jeans and cowboy boots. There were a few other stetsons about, and a lot of leather-fringed jackets.

The more Angela saw, the less she liked it. She smiled wryly at what Lewis would have thought if he could have seen her here.

Soon the music started and she brightened up momentarily. Cheerful Country and Western — just made for dancing. And she tried — she really tried. Oh, she could follow the moves well enough, but it just didn't feel right.

Maybe this was just the wrong place at the wrong time. After a couple of songs, she knew she had to escape.

When the music began again she made sure she was on the end of the line.

It was easy just to keep on sidling sideways until she was out of the door into the corridor.

Once there, she sat down on a bench and shook her head. It wasn't for her — but at least she'd given it a try.

Inside, the music stopped and there was some ragged clapping.

Benjamin David Goodman was born in Chicago in 1909, and grew up there. His parents couldn't guess that this jazz clarinettist and bandleader would come to be known as "The King Of Swing"!

Benny Goodman joined his local musicians' union aged only thirteen, and formed his first band in 1934.

The following year he took the band to, among other places, Los Angeles, and they became a huge hit.

He was respected as an excellent musician and soloist, and appeared in several films, including "The Big Broadcast Of 1937".

During his long career he went all over the world, including the Soviet Union in 1962.

He died in 1986.

Then the door opened and Mhairi appeared, looking worried — but Angela was ready. She held up her hands.

"Now, look, dear," she said gently, before her daughter could speak. "I know you meant well, but this really isn't my scene at all!"

"You've hardly tried!" Mhairi wailed in disappointment. "You've got to give it a proper go."

"No, I haven't," Angela said flatly. "I've come, I've seen, and now I'm going."

She patted her daughter on the arm.

"You stay, though — you enjoy it."

Mhairi sighed.

"Well, if that's what you want," she said resignedly. "But it's such a shame. I was sure you'd love it! I always have such a good time when I'm here — and everyone's so friendly."

She turned to go back into the hall, where the music had just started again.

Pictorial Press.

"Are you sure you'll be OK?"

Angela nodded.

"Of course! I'll get a taxi and I'll phone you tomorrow, Mhairi."

As Mhairi disappeared into the hall and the door swung shut behind her, Angela leaned back against the wall, worn out with keeping a cheerful face on for everyone else's benefit.

For a moment, she felt dangerously close to tears. Perhaps she needed some air.

ANGELA stepped outside and drew a deep breath. As she did so, she saw a taxi parked by the kerb. What a bit of luck!

She approached the car and saw, with some surprise, that it was Ben's.

"What are you still doing here?" she said, surprised.

"Waiting for you," he replied calmly. "I had a feeling you'd be back before long."

"What made you think that?"

He looked her straight in the eye, and once again she was caught unawares by that strange, delicious tingle down her spine.

"Not your scene," he said.

Angela sat down beside him.

"Do you know me that well?" she said curiously.

He shifted awkwardly in his seat.

"No — no — I just — well — like to be around . . ."

Angela reached out and touched his hand.

"Thank you," she said softly.

He looked embarrassed.

"No need for thanks!"

There was a pause.

"It's been difficult," Angela said, with an effort. "You know — after Lewis. You take someone for granted, almost, when they're always there for you, always around — it's only when they're gone you realise how much is missing from your life."

Ben nodded.

"Good friend to me," he said gruffly. "One of the best."

Angela smiled wistfully.

"Mhairi's right, though. Life has to go on — we all know Lewis wouldn't have wanted it any other way."

Ben agreed.

"Anyway," he said briskly, "I'd better take you home now!" He looked round the car.

"But haven't you forgotten something?"

Angela groaned.

"Oh, no! That stupid stetson!"

"Would you like me to get it for you?" he asked.

"Oh, no, really!" Angela laughed. "I didn't want to bring it. In fact, I didn't want to come at all. I think it was just the wrong time and certainly the wrong place!"

Ben took a deep breath.

"Maybe," he said. "Maybe not."

He hesitated.

"Look, lady — how's about us meetin' up, say, tonight, and sharing a hot dog and a soda at ma place, huh?"

Angela was taken aback.

"Could you say that in English?" she stuttered.

Ben turned scarlet.

"Don't know much about this sort of thing!" he said sheepishly. "I've got two left feet when it comes to romance!"

Before Angela could speak, Mhairi came running out of the hall, clutching the missing stetson. She seemed surprised to see Ben still there with her mother.

"I thought I'd missed you!" she said. "You forgot this. Look, I'm sorry about twisting your arm to come here today. What about if I stop by later with a bottle of wine to say sorry?"

Angela smiled.

"Sorry, sweetheart," she said cheerfully, "but I have a date with a hot dog and a can of soda!"

"Sorry?" Mhairi looked puzzled as Ben's face lit up with a big grin.

"I'll tell you later." Angela took the stetson from Mhairi and placed it at a jaunty angle on Ben's head. "But right now, we ought to be getting back to the ranch."

Mhairi stood waving as the taxi pulled away and drove off down the street. She suddenly felt lighthearted, for the first time since her dad died.

Maybe twisting Mum's arm to come along today hadn't been such a bad idea after all. ■

Following Tradition . . .

GENEVIEVE ESMERALDA PRICE sat on her great-grandad's lap and chortled up at him.

She looked very cute in the frilled dress and bonnet that her great-grandma, Joyce, had made at her mother's request.

Joyce smiled wryly to herself. True, she had enjoyed the challenge of making the tiny garments. And yes, she did privately nurture a preference for dressing babies traditionally, rather than in the modern colours and fabrics of today.

by Philippa Kent.

Illustration by Linda Worrall.

But Genevieve Esmeralda? Wasn't that taking things a little too far?

"I'm still not sure about her name," Joyce ventured. "They're both very pretty names, but it's a bit of a mouthful, having both of them together, don't you think?"

Trevor eased the baby into a more comfortable position and shot his wife a glance that clearly told her not to interfere.

"It's up to Caroline and Keith what they call her," he said. "I don't have a problem with either. Genevieve's no longer than Caroline."

"But Caroline's always been called Caro," Joyce said.

"Not by me she hasn't. I've always called her Caroline," Trevor said firmly. "Not that any of this makes any difference to me. Whatever they call this one, she'll always be my little lass, won't you?" He jiggled the baby up and down and she obligingly gurgled in response.

"She'll have trouble when she goes to school," Joyce persisted. "The other children will have nice easy names to learn to write, like Jane and Ann, while Genevieve . . . or is to be Esmeralda? Caro doesn't seem to have made her mind up yet . . ."

"She'll cope." Trevor was not to be drawn. "Bright as the proverbial button, she is. Besides, school's a long way off yet. Here, you take her. My arm's getting tired."

With a smile Joyce took the baby from him and carried her to her buggy to put her down for a nap. She had to admit this new-fangled buggy that cleverly trebled up as a car seat and a carrycot was a boon — far superior to the cumbersome prams and pushchairs of her day.

She wheeled the buggy out and parked it under the cherry tree. Mellow September sunshine washed the fields with golden light and Joyce looked round with contentment at the small garden, bright with autumn colour.

She was glad she and Trevor had built this bungalow for their retirement, just across the way from the baby's farmhouse home. Swallows were gathering on the roofs for their long flight across the ocean and Joyce smiled at the peaceful scene, waving to the little one's father who was crossing the yard to his tractor.

Despite the recent setbacks with farming, it was good to know that Keith and Caro were carrying on the family farm. Already Caro had put her own stamp on the house, updating the kitchen and replacing the old central heating unit with a modern system.

When the exciting news of the baby had first been announced and Caro began her preparations, Joyce fully expected a super-modern nursery to materialise in the bedroom under the eaves where she'd slept as a child.

Instead, she'd found pastel walls and natural pine furniture, with the wicker nursing chair brought down from the attic and refurbished.

"Why, this is lovely," Joyce had cried in delight.

"Glad you approve," Caro had said blithely. "Um, if you feel like getting the sewing machine out, Gran, I've ordered a Victorian-style cradle for the baby."

"You want me to make drapes and covers for it?" Joyce's voice was faint. "Any particular colour preference?"

"Oh, pink and white. It's a girl, after all. We might as well make the most of things. It could be a boy next time!"

Joyce had stared at her granddaughter and remembered the tough little pony-riding, tree-climbing child she had been — a tomboy to the last.

"Amazing what changes motherhood can bring," she commented later to Trevor.

Her husband, deep in his farming paper, rustled the pages and said what did she expect?

"Caroline's a stunner. Not everyone could look good in boiler suit and wellies, milking a herd of cows, but she manages to. Of course she'll go for frills and falderals for her little lass. It's only natural."

"I can't wait till her mother sees it all." Joyce chuckled. "Isla'll never believe it — and neither will Stephen."

Their daughter and son-in-law, who most certainly were not farmers, had followed the trend for retiring to the sun and were happily settled in Spain. But they were looking forward to travelling back over for the christening and seeing their first grandchild.

* * * *

The date had been set for October, when the harvest was safely over.

Out of mothballs came the family christening robe and shawl. Both were yellowed with age and Joyce looked at them doubtfully.

"Caro, pet, are you sure you wouldn't rather I made new ones? There are some lovely fabrics these days, and the yarn for knitting baby clothes is beautifully white."

Shrugging, the young mother hooked an errant strand of ash-blonde hair behind her ear.

"This gown's made of hard-wearing cotton. Let's give it a wash and see how it comes up. And this, too," she said, gently fingering the delicate filigree lace on the hand-knitted shawl. "I quite like the off-white look. It makes me think of our own flock out there."

"That figures," Joyce said, holding the shawl up to the light to check for any sign of moths. "This wool probably came from them in the first place."

"All the more reason to use the shawl for the christening then." Caroline grinned affectionately at her gran, and Joyce's heart melted.

"All right, we'll see what a good laundering can do," she promised.

Into the tub went gown, petticoats and shawl and, to everyone's delight, they came out looking as good as new.

Carefully hand-washed and pressed, the bygone outfit was wrapped in tissue paper and put aside in the nursery drawer, ready for the special day.

Joyce couldn't help wondering what the baby's mother would be wearing. Jeans and a jumper or a hygienic dairy boiler suit was all she ever saw Caro in these days. But she knew better than to mention her concerns to Trevor — he'd only tell her it was none of her business!

Besides, there was too much else to think about. What with all the to-ing and fro-ing to town to get herself and Trevor sorted with new clothes for the big day, not to mention helping Caro to organise the food and make the house ready for the guests, the time ran away with Joyce. All too soon the corn harvest was in, the old house sparkled and the grandparents arrived home from abroad.

Gradually, the other guests started arriving, too, aunts and uncles, cousins, friends, and the rooms rang pleasingly with chatter and laughter as everyone made preparations for church.

* * * *

It turned out to be a perfect day. Joyce was relieved to see that Caro turned up in a neat shift dress of warm autumn hues, her shining hair in a French pleat. The sun shone and everyone seemed to smile all day.

Despite her father's forecast to the contrary, Genevieve Esmeralda behaved with true decorum at the baptism. She didn't object to being handed to the rector and uttered not a squeal of protest at the icy quality of the font water. Clucked and fussed over the whole time, she beamed good-naturedly up at everyone during the feast that followed.

Isla was over the moon with her new granddaughter and proclaimed loudly that she'd never known such a good baby.

"You're a credit to us, Genevieve Esmeralda," she said.

Caro shot her mother a pained look across the white expanse of tablecloth.

"Oh, come on, Mum! You don't expect me to go shouting that across the fields, do you?"

"So what are we to call her?" Caro's father asked in some bewilderment.

Caro's gaze slid to her gran.

"It's Ginnie," she said, grinning.

A quiet sigh of relief escaped Joyce's lips. That's more like it, she thought. It's all very well having traditions, and it's lovely to see all the old things coming into their own again — the gown and shawl, the old-fashioned cot and frilly drapes — but somehow Ginnie seemed much more fitting as a name.

"So that's that sorted," Trevor murmured at her side. "The grandmother's happy with the baby, the mother's wearing a respectable dress and the great-gran can stop worrying about the baby's name. Now let's just get on and enjoy the little lass, shall we?"

"Absolutely," Joyce said, smiling. ■

Hook, Line And Sinker

by K. Paton.

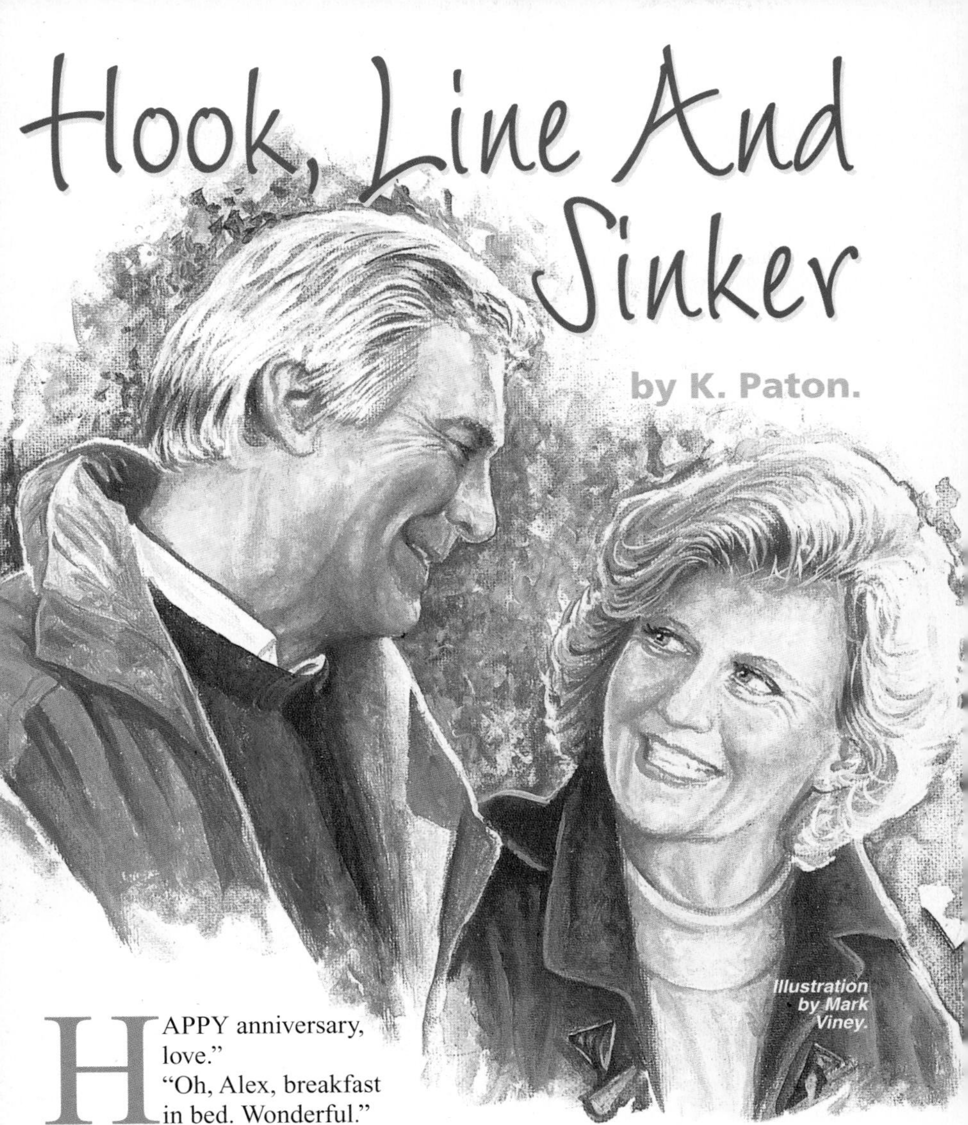

Illustration by Mark Viney.

"HAPPY anniversary, love."

"Oh, Alex, breakfast in bed. Wonderful."

"Well, it's not every day you celebrate thirty years of wedded bliss, is it?" Alex placed the tray carefully on the bed.

Poached egg on toast. My favourite. And a full pot of tea. It was a family joke that I needed at least six cups of tea in the morning before my brain could function properly.

"And is it?" I ate a piece of toast and sipped my tea.

"Is what it?"

"Wedded bliss. And just be careful how you answer."

"Right." Alex started pacing up and down the bedroom.

"What are you doing, love?"

"I'm thinking carefully before I answer you. I mean I wouldn't like to put my foot in it by saying something stupid now, would I? Something like bank robbers getting off with a lighter sentence."

"Alex!" I threw the pillow at him and started to laugh. Thirty years — I could hardly believe it. "You don't regret it, do you, love? I mean, it hasn't always been easy, has it?"

"Valerie, my darling, I have lots of regrets. But marrying you is not one of them."

I smiled. That was my Alex. Compliments were seldom given and even then I had to read between the lines.

"You're up early. Going somewhere?"

"Yes. I'm going fishing up at the lake. In fact, I wondered if you wanted to come with me? I mean, it is a beautiful day — we could take a picnic, and you've got plenty of books to read."

"Actually, it sounds great. Sitting by the water's edge, sipping champagne, eating caviare. What more could I ask for?"

"Yes, well, don't get carried away. It's more likely to be egg sandwiches and lukewarm tea. Still, it's a glorious day and I'm sure the fish will be biting. And I've got a new fly to try out."

"Ah. There's the real reason. Nothing at all to do with romantic picnics beside the lake. It's all about trying out a new fly. I might have guessed."

"Valerie! That's not true, and you know it."

"I know, love, I'm only teasing. Look, I'll get up and start the picnic, you start packing the car. OK?"

"Yes, ma'am." Alex clicked his heels, saluted and turned and ran out of the room, just before the other pillow hit the door.

He was a simple man, my husband. What you saw was what you got. As the saying goes, he had no side to him. This sometimes led people to think that he was a stupid man.

They soon found out how wrong they were. Alex was very intelligent. He had run his own business for the last twenty years, and you had to be clever to do that. Especially these days. No, my husband was no fool.

I put the kettle on to boil the eggs and started to butter some bread.

I HAD been working as a typist in a stationer's. I loved my job and had just started seeing Alex. He had plucked up the courage to ask me on a date and I had accepted.

I suppose he wasn't everyone's idea of a knight in shining armour, but he was kind and funny and he was just — Alex. Then Neil had arrived.

He had taken over as the chief salesman and had announced that he was going to make the company the biggest in the industry. This was a proud boast, but then Neil was a proud man.

The Ragamuffin

Some people smile at me, some people stare,
I'm all darns and patches —
a scamp, they declare,
But I like to be here, where
shoppers go by,
And though rather
cheeky, no sinner
am I.

And as for those
chestnuts, I don't
give a jot,
With my head in
the air, I pretend I
don't care
Whether I've tuppence
to buy some, or not.

I get on with most
folk, though children
are best,
But pompous
old peelers
I really detest.
I'd lob him a snowball, our Pete on the beat,
But then, he might nab me next time we meet.

Oh, the smell of those chestnuts is really so good,
The truth is, I'd buy some, if only I could . . .

— Kathleen O'Farrell.

He was also a very handsome man. All the girls immediately fell in love with him and I was no exception. I started to make comparisons between Alex and Neil, and Alex always seemed to be in second place.

Neil was more handsome and charming. He was stylish and confident. He just seemed to have everything. I decided to break it off with Alex. It wasn't fair to keep seeing him when all I thought about was Neil.

As usual, he was in his workroom fiddling about with feathers and bits of thread and fur. Alex lived and breathed fishing. Sitting at the side of a river, trying to catch a trout or two. Or if he was really lucky, trying to catch a salmon.

His dream was to open his own sporting goods shop, with the emphasis on fishing, of course.

"Hello, Alex." Oh, this was going to be so difficult. I could feel my heart pounding in my chest.

"Hello, Valerie! I didn't know you were coming round tonight. Just give me ten minutes to tidy up, then we can go out, OK? Hey, have I shown you my newest design?"

"No — what is it?" This wasn't right. I should just tell him.

"This is it. The Golden Dragon. What do you think?"

In his hand was a beautiful creation. A perfectly designed and crafted fly.

"It's beautiful, Alex, absolutely gorgeous. And so perfect. It looks so real." I had never really looked at any of Alex's creations before. I had never really been interested.

This was lovely, though. A work of art. When I told Alex this, he just smiled at me and put the fly down on the work table.

"Yes, it is pretty — but take a good look and see what's underneath all that beauty."

I stared at the table, not sure what to do or say.

"Umm, Alex — actually, I don't feel like going out. I think I'll just go home."

"Is everything all right, love? You're not ill or anything, are you?"

"No, no. I'm fine, just a bit of a headache. I'll see you tomorrow, OK?"

I MIXED the mayonnaise into the eggs and started making the sandwiches. I filled the Thermos and packed the hamper.

"You ready, love?"

"Yes, just coming." I smiled to myself, and wondered who else would spend their anniversary watching their husband try to catch fish? I must be mad.

I had taken Alex's advice and looked under all the glitz and glamour. Again, there was no contest. This time, though, the result had been different. Neil might have had all the style but Alex had all the substance.

I carried the hamper out to the car and put it in the boot.

"All set, love?"

"Yes — let's go catch some fish." ■

THE SNOW WISH

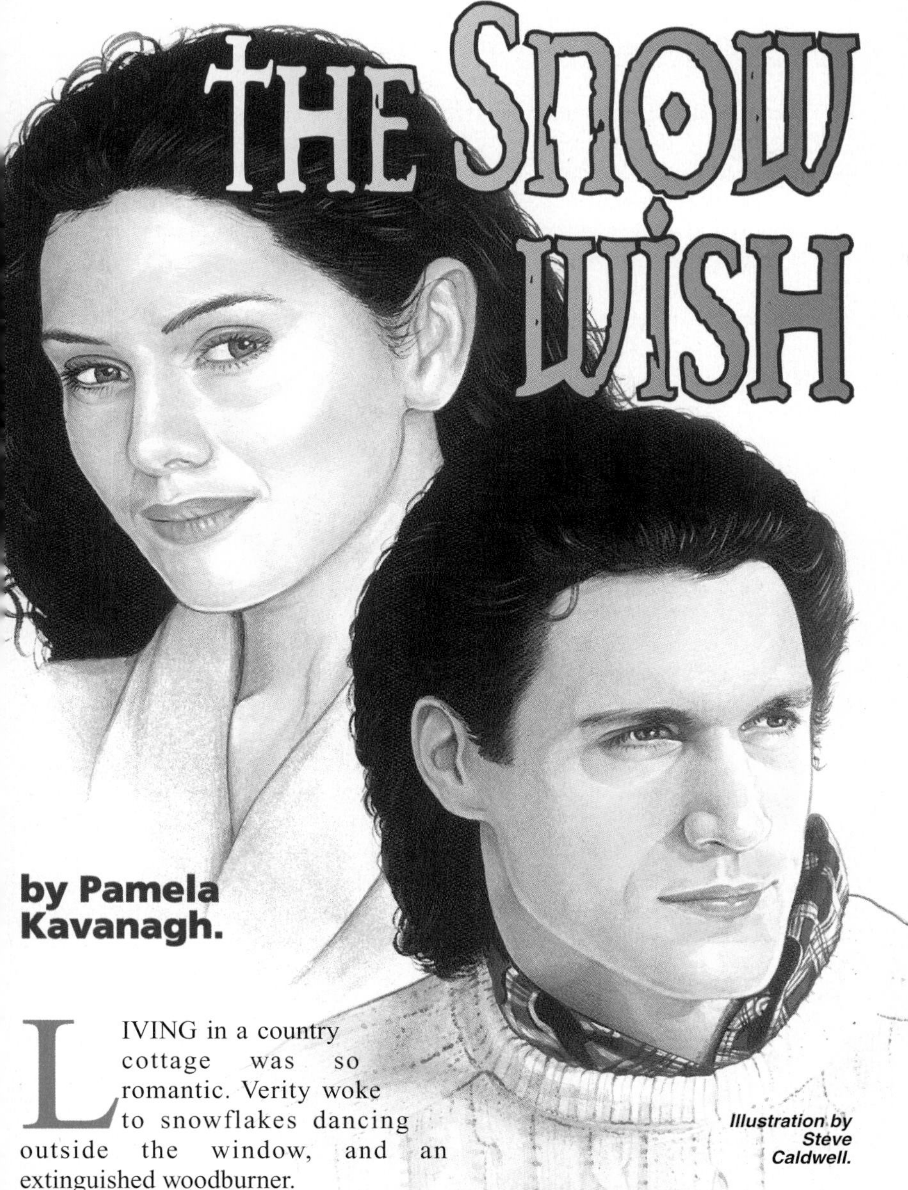

by Pamela Kavanagh.

Illustration by Steve Caldwell.

LIVING in a country cottage was so romantic. Verity woke to snowflakes dancing outside the window, and an extinguished woodburner.

Shivering in the icy air, she pulled on an extra jumper and set about clearing out the dead fire.

From his basket beside the cold hearth, her old black Labrador, Trapper, watched with reproach.

"Sorry," she told him. "Last night's wood must have been damp. Come on, boy. Let's fetch some dry stuff."

Tail thumping, Trapper padded after her to the back door.

Outside, the orchard and surrounding fields already had a covering of snow, and the lowering sky told of more to come.

Guy would have called her crazy to bury herself out here with no central heating and no near neighbours, but then Guy was an urban creature through and through, whereas Verity had always been a country girl at heart.

Reaching the woodshed, Verity eyed the diminished pile of fuel in the corner. She'd arrived at Holly Lodge a couple of months ago, full of plans for her honey farm, and on a strict budget.

Her first task had been to clear the tangled orchard of fallen timber, and stack it in here. Once the shed was full, she had considered her winter fuel sorted and focused on getting the builders in for the barn conversion.

How was she to know the dratted stove gobbled up wood at a rate of knots?

Verity gathered up a precious armful of logs and was heading back to the house when the post van drew up outside the gate.

"Snow's settling," the postman said, handing over her mail. "Hope you're well stocked up with fuel."

"I'm almost out," she admitted. "I didn't reckon on snow this early."

"Give John Talbot a ring – he's the logger up in the forest. John will fix you up with a load, no problem. He's in the book."

The red van vanished into the whirling snow. Verity called the dog and went indoors to open her mail — mostly bills. But there was the catalogue of beehives she had sent for — great. She put it behind the clock to be studied later and set about lighting the stove.

SOON it was crackling merrily. Verity made a mug of tea and some toast, and found the log man's telephone number.

No reply. Not even an answering machine! Typical, she thought.

It had been the same with the builder and the plumber. People obliged — eventually.

"We'll just have to go and find him," she said to Trapper. Pulling on her old waxed coat, she collected the dog's lead from the hook by the door and went outside.

The snow had stopped, and her breath hung in the cold air as she trudged down the lane to the forest. Through the trees came the sound of a chainsaw.

Verity followed the noise until she reached a low-roofed house and a yard stacked with timber. Standing with their heads over a field gate were two Shire horses.

"Oh!" Dog in tow, Verity went to talk to them. She stood stroking their noses as the snow began again, twirling gently down from a leaden sky.

"Have you made a wish?" a voice said, and Verity jumped.

The horses whickered a greeting. The man was youngish, snowflakes powdering his brown hair. Over his navy-blue boiler suit he wore a shabby all-weather coat.

"Hi," Verity said. "What did you mean by making a wish?"

"Make a wish on the first snow and it will come true — always supposing you have something special to wish for."

"A load of logs would do for starters. I'm looking for John Talbot?"

"You've found him." He smiled, right to the depth of his bright blue eyes.

Suddenly, unaccountably all of a fluster, Verity stared at him.

"I . . . I was expecting someone older," she babbled. "No-one seems to retire round here."

"It must be the outdoor life. My uncle was pushing eighty when he went — he had the woodyard before me.

"You're the new lady from Holly Lodge, aren't you? Rumour has it you're starting a honey farm."

"That's right."

"So what can I do for you?"

"I need logs. I tried to phone but there was no answer."

"Ah. I must get voicemail."

He sounded amused, and Verity made no reply. Once her honey business was up and running, all the basics would be seen to, and that included e-mail and a message service for potential customers.

At her feet, Trapper whined.

"Someone's ready for home." John Talbot looked down.

"Was it a full load of logs you wanted? That's cheaper than bags. Trouble is, I'll have to load up the truck, and . . ." He eyed the sky and grimaced.

"I don't mind helping," Verity said in desperation.

"Right. We'll have to use the horses — the truck's out of action at the moment." He gestured towards the barn where, parked beside a small tractor and some implements, there was a lorry with the bonnet ominously up.

By the time they had got Bonnie and Clyde between the shafts, and loaded up the cart with logs, Verity's muscles were screaming in protest. She'd quickly shed her coat and worked alongside the woodman, a sturdy figure in a washed-out jumper and blue jeans.

"Up you get." John helped her aboard the laden vehicle, and they went rumbling along the snowy track, icy flakes beading their lashes and whipping colour into their already glowing cheeks.

Trapper sat between them, quite relaxed, as if he had done this sort of thing all his life.

"Do you use the horses often?" Verity asked.

"For local trips, sure. Mostly I work them in the forest and some places are impassable for a tractor. That's when a horse and tackle comes in useful.

"Added to which, their fuel's renewable — it all makes environmental good sense."

"And I thought horse power was a thing of the past!"

The Old Lady

*Drawn to the brazier's
welcoming glow,
An old lady remembers, how
long, long ago,
She and her brothers would race
to the Square,
To see if the man selling
chestnuts was there.
With Saturday pennies to
spend, they would run,
Snowballing each other, all
mischievous fun.*

*But those days are over . . .
with eyes rather sad,
The lady looks round, and
espies a young lad,
A real ragamuffin, in clothes
worn and thin,
With dreadful old boots, that
would let water in.
He looks such a scallywag, so cheeky-eyed,
Yet the gentle old lady has moved to his side . . .*

*And into the boy's hand, so chill to the touch,
She slips several coppers — it's not very much,
But enough for hot chestnuts, two scoops at the least,
Why, young Ragamuffin is in for a feast!*

— Kathleen O'Farrell.

At the lodge, the whole process had to be repeated in reverse.

By the end of another hour, the woodshed was stacked with seasoned timber for which John, generously, charged her only half price.

"Let me know if you ever want a job," was his parting shot as the horses pulled away. "We'll make a yard lad of you yet!"

Verity blushed. Apart from her hair, which was long and curling, she knew she had very little claim to beauty. "Didn't make the most of herself" had been one of the insults Guy had hurled at her during that final row.

Never mind that she had vowed to go it alone; for a few brief hours she had enjoyed a taste of male company, so John Talbot's words stung.

GET a grip!" she told herself, gathering a generous armful of logs and heading for the house. "Have a bite to eat and a browse through that catalogue. Keep busy, and the ghosts will go away."

Generally it worked, but this time, despite putting in her order for the new hives and printing out a set of business cards, the hurt remained.

She stared out at the snow still speckling the evening sky. What was it he had said? Always make a wish?

"I wish I was more glamorous," she said impulsively, and then chided herself for a fool.

"Men! See if I care what they think!"

Next morning, when the rap on the back door turned out to be John, Verity was hard put to present her most welcoming face.

"Hi, there." He smiled. "I wonder if you could help? I need a part for the truck, and the local garage can't supply one. I noticed yesterday you had transport . . . I wonder if you'd mind running me to the suppliers in town?"

She took one look at the deep drifts of snow, and groaned.

"In this?"

"They'll be out with the snow plough before long. I'll stand you the petrol, so you won't be out of pocket."

"My van's diesel." Privately, Verity thought he had a bit of a cheek. It wasn't as if they were old pals, was it?

"Can't they deliver? You can ring them, or get them on the net."

"Haven't got round to a computer, but even so, they'd never deliver immediately, and I need to get that truck on the road. There are deliveries pending, the children's home, for one."

Verity hesitated. The least she could do was return the favour.

"OK," she said. "I'll get my coat."

In fact, the twenty-mile drive into town wasn't as bad as she'd imagined.

"The supplier is just off the high street," John said. "If you've any shopping to do, here's your chance."

They parked the van, arranged to meet up in an hour and suddenly Verity was alone with time to kill.

The village store took care of her basic shopping, so this was the first time in weeks she'd been able to wander at leisure through a shopping precinct.

At a department store, she bought cream for her work-roughened hands, and splashed out on an extra rich face moisturiser.

She was about to leave when she happened to glimpse herself in one of the full-length mirrors. Scruffy jeans, the polo neck of her old sweater just visible above the collar of her well-worn waxed coat, hair scraped unflatteringly back from her face . . .

What a sight, she thought . . . and then did what she had vowed not to do and headed for the women's clothing.

She came away considerably lighter of pocket, and without the serviceable cords and jumper she had gone in for.

In the sale she'd seen a dress in a soft blue jersey that flattered her figure and brought out the colour of her eyes. After weeks of living in working gear, it made her feel so feminine.

"I'll take it," she said to the assistant, and had to run all the way to the coffee shop where she had promised to meet John.

"Sorry I'm late," she panted, sinking into the seat beside him. "Did you get what you wanted?" Surreptitiously she slid the bag with the revealing logo under the table.

"I did, thanks. I'll have the truck on the road tomorrow. Cappuccino? Would you like a Danish pastry with it?"

"Just coffee, please." To her delight, the weeks of physical work had trimmed her down, as she'd discovered when she tried on the dress.

Over coffee they got chatting. John asked about the honey farm venture.

"My grandfather kept bees and it's something I've always wanted to do," Verity told him. "I saw Holly Lodge in the estate agent's window, and I was looking for a change of scene anyway."

"You're not from round here?"

"No. I'm from Winchester. I've never lived in the country before."

"And?"

"Well, I've survived so far. I had a problem with the builder, though. He never turned up when he said."

"I think that's pretty general." John laughed. "I saw work going on there. You've done a barn conversion?"

"Yes, my workshop. I got a grant for that. There's a kitchen and shelving and so on. I'm looking forward to the bees coming in the spring."

"I bet." John was intrigued. "Did you do a course on beekeeping?"

"Oh, I had to. I was teaching before. Primary."

"I've done a career switch as well. I was in computers."

"Oh!" Verity bit her lip. "What made you give it up?"

"Well, Uncle Jack left me the yard, and it was either sell up or take over.

"Besides, there were the horses. I promised the old boy I'd look after them.

My girlfriend had found someone else so there was only myself to consider."

"Me, too," Verity said in a low voice. "I was engaged, only it all went wrong."

"Better now than afterwards."

"Mm. I'm doing my own thing from now on. How long have you been in business?"

"Getting on for two years. Time I got the office side up to scratch, I suppose, though I rather enjoy poodling along the way my uncle did."

"Fair enough." Verity glanced at her watch, and groped for her bag. "Do you mind if we head back? Trapper will be wondering where I've got to, and there's the stove. The wretched thing goes out unless I'm there to feed it."

Verity dropped John and his purchases off at the yard and drove home.

Once there, she took the new dress out of the bag. Here in the cottage kitchen, it looked totally out of place.

What extravagance, Verity chided herself. What an utter waste of money!

She took the dress upstairs and hung it at the back of her wardrobe. And there it would stay.

THE snow remained, coming in fits and starts. Every day Verity had to clear a path to the woodshed and gate.

The hives arrived, but there was no point in assembling them until the weather improved. She spent the time painting the workshop walls and setting up the equipment, muffled up to her eyes in her warmest clothes and dreaming of spring. Never had it seemed so far off.

Sometimes John rumbled past in the newly repaired truck, or clopped by with the horses. Always, he waved and shouted a greeting.

It came as a shock when Mum rang to enquire what she would be doing over Christmas.

"Dad and I are going to Spain, as always." They enjoyed a winter break. "You're very welcome to come with us, darling."

"Thanks, Mum, but I can't. There's Trapper, and I don't fancy leaving the place unattended. With the snow there's always the worry about burst pipes.

"When is it anyway?"

"Thursday week. Don't tell me you didn't know."

Verity mumbled something about time running away with her, and made a panicky decision to go Christmas shopping.

She'd just put the phone down when it rang again.

"Hi. It's John."

"Hi, there," Verity replied cautiously.

"How's things? Woodburner behaving?"

"So-so. It's a hungry monster — doesn't half race through the fuel!"

"There's a way of regulating the draught. Do you want me to take a look at it for you?"

"Please. I'd be grateful."

There was a pause.

"Look. I'm ringing on the off chance you'll come to my rescue again." John said. "Don't be afraid to say no if it's not convenient. Do you know about the Christmas Revels?"

"I heard it mentioned in the shop the other day. Isn't it a village tradition?"

"Right. It starts with a procession — the kids go in fancy dress and there's a prize for the most unusual. The horse folk do up their mounts or pony and traps for the occasion.

"I take my outfit, and that's my problem. I'm hopeless at thinking up ideas. And as for dressing the cart — I wouldn't know where to start."

"You want me to do it for you?" Verity said.

"Well, you were a teacher. They're a pretty inventive crowd, if memory serves me right! It can be anything bar Santa Claus. Someone's already earmarked for that.

"We parade through all the local villages. It takes a few hours —"

"We?"

"Of course! You're in on the act as well. After the parade there's a kids' party in the village hall, and then a dance and buffet for the adults in the evening. It's usually good fun."

"You're asking me to come with you?" Verity was startled.

"Of course I am. What is this? Are you always so prickly?"

"I'm in shock, that's all! I'm sure you can find someone more decorative to take." Verity's mind whirled. Her hair was a mess. And what would she wear?

"Come on!" John said. "It's the cart that needs decoration, not the girl. It'll

Glen Clova, Angus

FROM the Braes of Angus just behind Kirriemuir, the Grampian foothills appear to roll down to the town's doorstep. Kirrie's other name, of course, is the Gateway to the Glens.

The entrances to Glens Isla, Prosen and Clova are all a few minutes' drive away. You can almost do a circular tour of Glen Clova. It does end at Braedownie, but unless you feel like walking, you just need to turn and

come back, not necessarily by the same road.

At Milton of Clova, a wee village, you cross the Gella Bridge and return by the road on the other side of the water. The river, meandering along the bottom of the glen, never very far from sight, is the South Esk. It rises high in the Grampians and meets the North Sea at Montrose.

Don't expect to view Clova Castle, near the upper end of the glen just beyond Milton of Clova, however. Time has not been kind and little remains of the 16th-century tower, its four-foot-thick walls sadly reduced to rubble.

give you a chance to show off that frock you bought in town."

Verity got her breath back with difficulty.

"How did you know?"

"I don't miss much. Did you make a wish, by the way?"

"I did, actually. Did you?"

"Oh, yes. What did you wish for? Ten swarms of honey bees?"

"If you tell a wish it doesn't come true."

"Sorry, teacher!" He chuckled. "Is it on?"

"Thanks — I'd like to come, and I'll have a think about the float. When is this, by the way?"

"Saturday."

"What?" Verity yelped. "But that's the day after tomorrow!"

"Right. Any props you need, tinsel and stuff, ring me and I'll run into town for it."

"In my van, I suppose?"

"Wrong! I've invested in a set of wheels. Couldn't take the honeybee lady to the ball in the truck, now could I? Cheers, Verity."

"Bye, John." She was laughing as she rang off, but quickly sobered. What could they go as? There was no time for the complicated masterpieces she had created at school . . .

In the end, the answer came to her just like that.

She rang John back.

"That was quick."

"Wasn't it just? We go as Logger and his Lad, from the turn of the last century. We load up the cart as usual, and cut boughs of holly to decorate it. There's plenty in my garden, and we could do up sprigs to hand out.

Mistletoe, too, if you can find some."

"Leave that to me! There are some old working clothes of Uncle Jack's here somewhere. I should be able to squeeze into them — but who's playing the lad?"

"I am. It was you who gave me the idea. You said I'd make a good yard lad."

Embarrassment sizzled over the line.

"I did? Me and my big mouth! Hope you didn't take it personally."

"Oh, I got over it." Verity smiled. "So what do you think?"

"I think it's brilliant. I might nip over now for the holly, if that's OK? I can take a look at that stove while I'm at it.

"And remember, this isn't a West End performance. You don't have to go overboard with the characterisation! Don't go cutting off that glorious mane of yours."

"I'll bundle it into a cap," Verity said.

THEY made a striking pair aboard the holly-decorated cart, John in his high-necked jacket, breeches and gaiters, a wide-brimmed hat over his dark hair. Older members of the village were heard to declare he was the spit of his uncle Jack.

Verity wore her black cords and gansey. With her hair hidden and her cheeks daubed with eyebrow pencil, she looked the part, as did Trapper, who came along for the ride, a festive red ribbon on his collar.

Bonnie and Clyde's harness bells jingled merrily as they clopped along, bringing up the rear of the procession. On the cart was a traditional Yule log which John had been up at the crack of dawn to load.

The sun shone on the jolly procession as it wound onward, through villages and between white, sparkling fields, the horse folk in their decorated traps and carriages laughing and waving, the children in their fancy dress making slides on the ice.

Heading the procession was Santa with his attendant elves — four small persons hand-picked for the job and enjoying it immensely.

All the children received a prize. The overall winner, a pretty child dressed as a Christmas rose, had something extra special in her parcel.

The party was riotous.

"School parties were never like this!" Verity sagged over the piano, on which she had hammered out every seasonal tune known to her. "I don't think I've got any energy left for dancing tonight!"

"Go on," John said. "You'll get your second wind."

She was home in plenty of time to get ready. A hot shower put paid to the stage make-up. Her hair, newly trimmed and shampooed, was coiled up on the top of her head.

The blue dress, when she slipped it on, was gratifyingly loose over the hips. She slid her feet into strappy shoes, threw a spangly shawl across her shoulders and scrutinised herself.

All that work had brought colour to her cheeks and a spark to her eyes. Her figure, honed by constant exercise, was trim now, rather than sturdy.

"You'll do," she told herself with a nod.

She had stoked up the stove and was feeding Trapper by the time John arrived in his new hatchback. Smiling, he escorted her into the village hall, where a band was playing traditional jazz.

She met his eyes, and thought she saw admiration there. Or was it merely appreciation of her efforts? She had given up her time on his behalf, after all, and time was a precious commodity when you were self employed.

The band struck up a Charleston.

"Let's show them how it's done," John said.

He whirled her on to the floor, and her doubts and insecurities melted away as they danced until they could dance no more. Then they collapsed, breathless and laughing, at the nearest table. John went for drinks, and afterwards they danced again.

The buffet did the WI proud, everything from cold meats and salads to melt-in-the-mouth pastries, and a vast raspberry and cream trifle.

It was well after midnight when the last waltz was called, and getting on for one when John stopped the hatchback at Verity's gate.

The night was brilliant with stars. Outlined against the orchard fence, the newly positioned row of hives glistened with the frost.

Verity sighed. It had been a long day, and she was achingly tired.

John turned to her.

"Thank you for everything. I could never have managed without you," he said formally.

"The yard lad."

His teeth flashed white in the darkness.

"Come on, you'd never be mistaken for a lad! You look stunning tonight. You were the loveliest there."

"Thank you." Then Verity recalled her wish. "It was my plea to the first snow. I asked for glamour, and for once I got it."

"You've got more than glamour, you've got style! My wish was granted, too. At least, I think so.

"I was chain-sawing when the snow began. I asked for something momentous to happen, and blow me, when I got back to the yard there you were, chatting away to the horses as if your life depended on it.

"What's more, you don't balk at hard work, and loading logs is strenuous business. I've waited a long time for a girl like you."

"I'm no girl, not any more." Verity's heart was hammering in her ribs.

"You are to me." John smiled at her. "I hope you've kept Christmas free, because we're celebrating it together."

And taking her in his arms, he drew her to him and kissed her. ■

I WAS doing a bit of mending in the lounge when a heart-felt sigh made me look up.

Liam, my five-year-old grandson, sat on the patio bench just outside the open french windows, his shoulders slumped as though from the weight of the world.

Granny's Memory Tin

By Sandra Beswetherick

Illustration by Sally Rowe.

I set aside my needle and thread and Liam's shirt — the one that needed yet another lost button to be re-sewn — and joined my grandson, sitting down beside him on the bench.

"Hi, Liam. I thought you were helping Grandpa in his workshop?"

Liam folded his arms stoutly across his chest and remained silent.

His mum had been advised by her doctor that she mustn't exert herself too much during this, the last week of her pregancy. So she and Liam's dad entrusted him, for a time, into the care of his grandpa and granny.

I tried to put my arm around Liam's shoulder, but he leaned away from my embrace.

"What's the matter?" I asked, although I suspected he was homesick.

The novelty of helping Grandpa build birdhouses, of watering Granny's garden — Granny, too, on occasion — and playing with Brennan, our Irish setter, had worn a bit thin. Four whole days and nights without his parents must have seemed a very long time, I'm sure.

"Nobody loves me," Liam finally answered, his head bowed, his bottom lip protruding. "Mum and Dad don't love me."

I suppressed a smile. In a child's small world, most problems seemed to distill into this very crucial one.

"You know your mum and dad love you, Liam."

I'd stopped explaining his mum's need for rest and the prospect of a new baby sister.

His most recent response was that he should be enough for his parents to love, and they didn't need another one, especially not this baby sister who was already causing trouble.

"You know Grandpa and I love you, too." I extended my arm again, but he slid along the bench out of my reach.

At this safe distance, he examined me, his head tilted imperiously.

"Prove it," he said. "I want concrete proof."

I looked at him, aghast. Where had he learned that expression, and did he know what it meant?

"Concrete proof?" I repeated. "Concrete proof that I love you?"

He nodded, once.

"Hmmm," I answered, stalling for time. Concrete proof of love. I examined my left hand, the engagement ring and wedding band on my finger. Concrete proof? I opened that hand and revealed the object that lay within.

I couldn't help but smile.

"I have concrete proof, Liam. In my treasure tin."

"Treasure tin?" he asked, his eyes lit with sudden interest.

HE followed me into the house, down the hallway and into my sewing room. I took from the top shelf of my sewing cupboard a small, shiny, silver tin.

Liam and I sat down on the daybed. I set the tin between us and removed the lid. The soft lilac scent of my grandmother's powder, originally stored in this tin, escaped, even after these many years.

How many families still kept such a tin in this modern, throw-away world?

It was a family heirloom, of sorts, I supposed, originating from a need for thrift, then passed from one generation to the next, with each generation contributing to the collection.

Liam dipped his hand into the tin.

"It's only buttons," he said in disappointment.

He selected a small button of cut crystal and held it to his eye.

"Is this a diamond?" he asked hopefully.

I laughed.

"No, it's not. But it's just as precious to me. It's a button from my grandmother's — and your great-great grandmother's — wedding dress. She was a quite a remarkable lady. She . . ."

"Oh," Liam said, unimpressed.

Then the button, as he held it up, caught a ray of sunlight from the window and cast a small, shimmering rainbow on the wall.

"Cool!" Liam exclaimed, and he chased the rainbow around the room.

I chose another button, a silver one embossed with two fire axes, handles crossed.

"This button is from your Great-uncle Albert's firefighter's uniform."

Liam returned the crystal button to the tin and accepted the silver one.

"Uncle Albert was a firefighter?"

"Oh, yes, he was. He fought lots and lots of dangerous fires. He's my older brother, you know, and he's always been a hero to me.

"Maybe you'll be a hero to your little sister."

"Maybe," Liam said, in a tone that was carefully casual. He put the button back, searching for another.

"Except, I'm going to be an astronaut."

"Wow!" I said and wondered if an astronaut's space suit came with buttons.

Arundel, Sussex

ARUNDEL is a real country town, set near the gently rolling South Downs country Kipling loved, yet just a few miles inland from "dear old Sussex-by-the-Sea". The town got its name from *hirondelle*, the French word for swallow.

This goes back to William the Conqueror, who commanded his trusted lieutenant, Roger

de Montgomery, to build a castle at Arundel. When Roger had duly made sure local government had a focus, he ended up with an earldom for his pains.

The title now belongs to the heir to the Dukedom of Norfolk and the castle is a tourist attraction. Reassuringly, Arundel doesn't have any typical high street stores. Instead, there's a wonderful array of antiques and bric-à-brac shops which you definitely won't be able to resist!

J. CAMPBELL KERR.

Together we found a brass button from the soldier's uniform my father wore, a nurse's pin that belonged to my mother, a button from the fancy vest Cliff wore when he proposed, and a pink, satin-covered button from Liam's mum's first party dress.

"I've always kept buttons from the clothes of all the people I love and treasure. That's the reason I call it my treasure tin."

"Hey!" Liam exclaimed, his eyes lighting up. "I remember these."

He balanced on the palm of his hand four small buttons each in the shape of a sleeping cat.

"They're from my favourite cat pyjamas when I was little!"

"Well!" I said in mock surprise. "I wonder what they're doing in my treasure tin?"

I caressed one small cat button with a fingertip. Liam looked up at me, then puckered his face into a impish grin.

I must admit I'm amazed, sometimes, by the leaps of logic a child's mind can make.

"Concrete proof!" Liam declared. "My cat buttons in your treasure tin mean you love and treasure *me*."

I nodded.

Liam carefully restored his cat buttons to my tin, then threw his arms around me.

"I love you, too, Granny." ■

The Christmas Box

by Pauline Kelly.

CASSIE was like a child where Christmas was concerned. The very thought of carols and tinsel was enough to give her a lift of pure happiness. So, when she was clearing out gran's house prior to — possibly — putting it on the market, and came across an old wooden box of festive decorations in the attic, she gave a little cry of delight.

Her pleasure was short-lived. As she lifted out the dusty streamers and garlands, they all but crumbled to bits in her hands. The lanterns were no better, their colours faded, and the ribbons of gilt and silver that had once gleamed magically would never do so again.

Cassie put them on the growing pile of rubbish destined for the bin, and took a peep inside the battered cardboard containers at the bottom of the box. They held Christmas tree decorations, all blessedly intact.

Wafer thin and fragile, the golden balls, silver stars and angels' trumpets in magical colours glittered up at her. There was even a fairy for the top of the tree.

Cassie picked her up. The little doll had a china face and faded golden curls. Her cloth body was dressed in hand-stitched layers of frothy off-white lace. Gauzy wings, embroidered with tiny glass beads, sprouted from her shoulders.

Wintry sunshine filtered in through the small skylight, throwing drowsy rays into the dusty, shadowed corners of the attic and illuminating the ranks of heavy old furniture Gran had stashed away up here. Cassie picked up the doll and sank into a creaking old rocking-chair that had seen better days.

The decision on whether or not to sell the house was so difficult, especially now she and Morgan had fixed their wedding date for next June and needed somewhere to live!

Weighing up all the pros and cons of keeping or selling Gran's tall Victorian home was bewildering. Situated conveniently close to the town where they both worked, yet affording wonderful views and easy access to the fells in which they loved to walk, it couldn't have been better placed.

On the down side, it needed new electrics, a new kitchen, new heating . . . the list went on and on. Plus, there was the added complication of Gran having left the house to Cassie and her sister, Imogen, between them.

"We'd have to buy Immie out," Cassie had said doubtfully to Morgan, way back in the summer. "Then there's the cost of refurbishing to consider. It might be best to sell, Morgan. I think that's what Immie wants to do anyway."

Morgan, a man who liked to keep his options open, suggested they took things one step at a time.

"Let's clear out the rooms first, then get it valued and go from there?"

WELL, the lofty rooms now stood bare and echoing. There was just the attic to sort out, and then, Cassie supposed, they should find an estate agent.

She sighed. Try as she might, she was no nearer to making up her mind now about selling than she had been six months ago.

Imogen was happy to go along with whatever Cassie wanted, but Morgan was fast running out of patience with her indecision, and last night he had finally lost his temper.

"For goodness' sake, Cassie! I know I told you not to be too hasty, but this is ridiculous! If you want to keep the place, that's fine. We'll cut back on our wedding expenses and plough the money into the house instead.

"We'll just get the basics sorted out for now. The house isn't going to fall down around us. We can live in it meanwhile, and do the rest as we go along."

"But that'll take ages!" she'd protested.

"Not necessarily. We could do a lot of it ourselves. It might be fun."

"Depends what you mean by fun."

"Oh, come on, Cassie! Try to be positive for once."

Cassie was silent. It would be much less hassle to sell up, she thought. They could buy one of the new bungalows on the development just off the ring road and get on with their lives. Having children was high on their list of priorities, and how could you cope with babies when your house was being rebuilt around you?

Illustration by John Hancock.

"I don't know," she'd said woodenly, and Morgan had got up and slammed out.

Cassie sighed, leaned back in the chair, and started to rock. She hated being at odds with Morgan. It was all her fault for being so indecisive.

"I don't blame Morgan for losing his rag, I really don't," she whispered to the tiny doll in her hands. "What shall I do for the best?"

The doll gazed up at her with a blue, unblinking stare. Creak, creak went the rockers of the old chair, and soon Cassie felt her eyes grow heavy . . .

"ME! Me! I want to put the fairy on the top! Please, Papa!"

The little girl wore a frilly dress tied round the waist with a broad sash. She jumped up and down in excitement, her dark ringlets bobbing. Laughing, the tall man scooped her up in his arms, sat her across his shoulders and approached the tree.

"There, Sarah. Can you reach? Here, let me help. Dear me, this fairy's frock is a bit worse for wear. It's all rags and tatters! Never mind, there she is, flying on the very top branch."

"Yes! See, Mama — look at Fairy."

From the sofa by the fire where she lay, with a multi-coloured shawl across her legs, the young woman smiled.

"Yes, sweetheart. How pretty the tree is looking, to be sure."

The man set the child tenderly on her feet, and turned to the small boy in the sailor suit and button boots.

"Now it's Jack's turn. What would you like to put on the tree, Jack? The toy soldier? Very well. Splendid!"

The fir tree stood tall in the corner of the parlour, its spreading boughs glittering with baubles and silvery chains, a slim candle tied with bows of ribbon tipping each branch, and the fairy in gauzy flight on the top.

The two children stood gazing rapturously at the tree, their dimpled hands clenched in joyful anticipation of the joys in store.

And then the door opened to admit Nanny.

"Excuse me, sir, madam. Time for nursery tea. Master Jack, Miss Sarah, come along. You shall see Mama and Papa later."

"Thank you, Nanny."

The children were ushered out and the door closed behind them. The woman rose from the couch, and immediately the man went across to her and took her hands.

"My dearest love," he said, "how are you feeling?"

"Very well indeed, thank you. I was thinking — that poor little fairy would look all the better for a new gown! I shall have to see what I can find in my needlework bag. A bit of lace and some net for wings, and the tree will have a fairy to be proud of.

"Just picture Sarah's face when she sees it. The child will think it's magic!"

He laughed gently.

"My dearest love. I can't tell you how happy you have made me."
"And you me."
"We have everything to be thankful for. We have each other, the children —"
"And this house. Do not forget that — it's such a happy house!"
"Indeed it is. How the time has flown! Christmas again — our anniversary."
"Yes. Oh, I do so love Christmas, don't you? The parties, the dressing up, the carols and all the good fare — oh, I cannot wait! I vow I am as bad as the children!"

She gave a delicious little peal of laughter that was suddenly quashed as her husband's lips came down lovingly on hers . . .

CASSIE woke with a start. Morgan was shaking her gently.
"Hey, Cassie, wake up. Are you OK?"
"I . . . of course." Confused, Cassie stared around her at the dusty attic and Morgan's familiar if slightly troubled face. "But what are you doing here?"
"I came to say sorry. I thought I'd find you here." From behind his back he whipped out a bunch of freesias, and presented them to her with a flourish.
"Oh, lovely. My favourite." She buried her face in the delicate blooms, breathing in their sweetness. Morgan wasn't exactly the demonstrative type and she felt the choke of foolish tears. "Thank you."
"I was wrong, Cassie. I shouldn't have blazed out the way I did. I'd had one of those days. The car wouldn't start, the boss was out of sorts at the office . . ."
"And I put the tin lid on it, as Gran would have said!"
They both laughed, and then Morgan caught sight of the doll in Cassie's lap.
"Hey, what's this?"
She showed him her find, then bit her lip. The dream was already beginning to fade, as dreams do. Sarah . . . hadn't that been the little girl's name? She'd been so sweet with her frilly dress and ringlets!
Gran's name had been Sarah, but that meant little — it was a family name.
Suddenly, Cassie's mind was made up.
"Morgan, let's keep the house. After all, it's been in the family for generations. It seems wrong to let it go. Gran would have loved us to live here and turn it into a proper home, the way it used to be."
"Children playing, dogs asleep on the rug, good cooking smells coming from the kitchen?" Morgan grinned. "Sounds all right to me!"
Cassie put the fairy back in the box. Next Christmas, they'd have a real tree to show off all the decorations.
"Lots of nice old stuff up here," Morgan remarked, glancing round. "Old houses need traditional furniture to look their best. Shall we take these back with us?" He picked up the box and tucked it under his arm. "Your Christmas box," he quipped, smiling. "I love you."
He dropped a glad-we're-friends-again kiss on her lips. And that, in Cassie's opinion, was the best Christmas box ever! ■

Let Nothing

by Kate Thompson.

IT had seemed like a good idea when, during a heatwave in July, I suggested we spend an old-fashioned Canadian Christmas at our cottage. Our summer cottage.

"Are you sure?" Bryce, my husband, looked at me dubiously. "The cottage is pretty basic, Liz."

"It'll be an adventure," I said grandly. "We'll be like pioneers."

Both of my children, fourteen-year-old Chris and eight-year-old Alisa, had been reluctant to leave Ottowa to go to the cottage for Christmas.

The cottage was fine in the summer, they told me, when it was warm and all their friends were there. But in winter? Chris looked positively bewildered.

"Why?" he asked succinctly.

"We'll be like pioneers," I repeated. It was fast becoming my mantra.

I had an image of a fairyland Christmas, everything rustic and beautifully decorated, far from the materialism of the festive season that was so rampant in the city. My children weren't convinced, and I wasn't sure my husband was either.

My enthusiasm buoyed us along, however, and we drove to the cottage on December 20. I for one was in anticipation of a truly magical Christmas holiday.

Silver Lake looked eerily beautiful under a thick blanket of snow. Gone were the fleets of rowing boats and canoes, the swimmers and water skiers. The only sign of life was a few ice-fishing holes in the lake. All of the other cottages were boarded up for the winter.

These were summer cottages, you see, not generally meant for winter habitation. There was no central heating and very little insulation, not to mention no running water in winter, in case the pipes froze. As Bryce had said, things would be basic.

"It's freezing," Chris moaned. He stood in the centre of the living-room, shivering in jeans, baseball cap and his favourite sweatshirt.

"We'll be fine once we get the fire going," I told him confidently.

I'd brought some electric heaters for the bedrooms, so I knew we wouldn't literally freeze, although at the rate the temperature was dropping we might come close.

"Why don't you find some suitable clothes? I packed your parka and your waterproofs."

Grumbling, Chris went to find them.

Alisa was looking far more cheerful than her brother.

"It's just like a fairy tale, Mummy! Everybody else is lost!"

Actually, everyone else was far more sensible than we were, snuggled up in centrally heated homes in the city.

There was a reason why the first weekend of May was generally considered to be the time when everyone opened their cottages for the summer. More to the point, there was a reason why people closed their cottages for the winter. It was cold.

You Dismay . . .

Illustration by Harry Norstrand.

"Still think this is a good idea?" Bryce teased as he brought in all our luggage from the car. In addition to our clothes, I had packed all the trimmings for Christmas: ornaments and decorations, the food for Christmas dinner — and, of course, presents.

"Absolutely."

I BELIEVED it, too, as we ate supper that night. There was a cheery blaze in the fireplace, and the electric heaters made our bedrooms if not warm, then at least less freezing.

Supper was a beef stew I had brought from home, and we all tucked in eagerly, the cold making us hungry.

"Tomorrow we can get a Christmas tree," I enthused.

"And, Chris, you can clear some of the snow off the lake — the ice must be a foot thick. Perfect to skate on."

Chris brightened considerably.

"I brought my hockey stick," he said with something almost resembling excitement.

"Maybe Dad and I could hit the puck around."

"Sure," Bryce replied agreeably.

"And Alisa can help me decorate the cottage." I smiled at them all, feeling proud and happy that this was coming off, that we were able to enjoy a rustic Christmas after all.

That night, after the children had gone to bed, Bryce and I stood on the front porch, gazing at a world cloaked in whiteness.

"It hardly seems like the same place," I said softly, even my whisper carrying in the perfect stillness. In the summer, Silver Lake was crammed with cottagers and daytrippers, drippy ice-creams and picnic baskets.

The hum of motorboats and the creak of oars, mingled with the ringing laughter of children, was a constant background noise for three long, hot months.

But now, the only sound was the creak of the ice shifting, and the whisper of a breeze on the snow, ruffling its pristine surface like a huge invisible hand smoothing a blanket. The sky was inky black with the stars standing out as bright pinpricks, the moon a sliver of silver.

"It's beautiful," Bryce whispered back. "I'm glad we came."

Everyone began to question that sentiment over the next few days.

First, of course, there was the lack of running water. I had brought plenty of bottled water for drinking, but for any other purpose snow had to be melted in pots on the stove. A laborious process, especially if you wanted enough water for a bath.

"We're all going to stink by the end of the week," Bryce informed me cheerfully. "And I think I'll forget about shaving."

I forgot about my hopes for a bath after calculating that it would take roughly twenty pots of melted snow before I had even a few inches of water in the tub. I'd be lucky if I was able to have a bath before we left at that rate.

Besides the lack of running water, there was of course the inescapable cold. I had forgotten how cold it could be in the woods.

"It's just as cold in Ottawa," Bryce told me with his usual irritating good cheer. "It's just that we have heating in Ottawa."

The fireplace warmed the living-room quite nicely, and the stove managed to keep the kitchen from freezing. The bedrooms, however, suffered. Bryce and I flipped a coin to see who would have to get into bed first.

"Since I'm a gentleman," he said when I'd lost, "I'll do it."

The sheets were freezing, you see. Bryce jumped in, pulling the covers over his head, and warmed the sheets up at least a little bit before I crawled in. I lay there, shivering, trying not to move even the tiniest bit lest I encounter a patch of freezing blanket. We slept like that the whole night, as still as statues, on our tiny bit of warmed space.

Still, I did my best to keep up my good cheer. Chris and Bryce spent the entire morning and a good part of the afternoon shovelling enough snow off the lake to make a rink big enough for two professional ice hockey teams.

Meanwhile, Alisa and I baked cookies and made paper chains to hang on the tree we would get as soon as Bryce and Chris had finished their shovelling. I hummed Christmas carols as I worked, feeling happy that we had come to the cottage for Christmas.

Since it was dark by the time Bryce and Chris had finished, we decided to get the tree the next day.

"Plenty of time," Bryce said, "and plenty of trees."

"And we can play ice hockey tomorrow, too," Chris said, his voice once again bordering on the enthusiastic. "Girls against the boys!"

I raised my eyebrows.

"But Alisa and I don't have hockey sticks."

Chris shrugged.

"You can use brooms."

I caught Bryce's eye and stifled a laugh.

"Fair enough," I agreed. I was sure Alisa and I would get clobbered, but perhaps that was Chris's aim.

THE temperature dropped that night, quite dramatically. We tucked Alisa and Chris up with hot-water bottles, put on as much warm clothing as we could, and hopped into bed, shivering.

"Nothing like being pioneers, eh?" Bryce whispered in my ear as he put his arms around me.

"Oh, stop it," I muttered. With the temperature at forty below zero and dropping, I was not in the mood to be teased.

The next morning the windows were covered with frost and even the dregs in our coffee cups from the night before had frozen. Even worse, a good foot of snow had fallen.

Chris gazed out of the frost-encrusted window, his expression utterly bereft.

"My ice rink!" he wailed, before his expression became grim and closed. "This place stinks! I hate it here!"

With that pronouncement, he slammed into his bedroom. I exchanged worried glances with Bryce.

"Can't you shovel it off again?"

Bryce sighed.

"A whole foot of snow . . . maybe. Not today, though. It's too cold to go outside for that long anyway."

"What?" I squawked. "What about our Christmas tree?"

"Liz." Bryce's voice was gentle. "There are at least twelve inches of snow on the ground, and last time I looked we didn't have a snow plough. We're not going anywhere."

"No tree!" Alisa cried, her face screwing up in disappointment. Then she burst into tears, which was exactly what I felt like doing.

Reality sank in at last. No rink, no Christmas tree, no shopping for food even. Fortunately I had brought enough supplies to last us, but I had been counting on at least one shopping trip for extras and treats.

CABIN fever set upon us quickly. Chris would have preferred to sulk in his bedroom, but it was too cold. He huddled by the fire instead, listening to his CD player so loudly that we could hear the tinny sound of the music through the headphones.

Bryce buried his nose in a book, and I played Chinese checkers with a rather subdued Alisa. By mid-afternoon, we were all snapping at each other.

Dinner was just tinned soup and bread, since I was afraid of using up our food supplies. Goodness knew how long we'd be snowed in!

Chris and Alisa slunk off to bed, both looking as if their whole world had caved in.

"This was a terrible idea," I told Bryce as we got ready for bed. We were both shivering, trying to jump into our pyjamas as quickly as possible.

"Christmas is going to be ruined, and we may have even put our children's lives in danger." I poked my head through the top of my flannel pyjama top and stared at him miserably. "It's all my fault."

"Hey." Bryce put his hands on my shoulders. "Let's not give up quite so easily. We're pioneers, remember? No-one's in danger, first of all. The roads will be cleared within a few days and we can hold on until then. It's about as cold as it can get, and we're surviving. And thanks to this jolly lumberjack —" he flexed his biceps, grinning "— we have plenty of firewood!"

I managed a small smile.

"But the children hate it. Chris is about as grim as death."

The Parents

They seem so close in every way, two halves that make
a whole,
As round the Square, so happily, Father and Mother stroll.

And their talk is all of
Christmas, of how lovely
it will be
With all the candles
blazing on their
splendid, greenwood
tree,
And eagerly they
recollect the
presents they have
bought,
The hobby-horse, the
humming-top, toy
soldiers, and a fort.

And for the children's
party they have
planned a big
surprise,
The little ones will
love it — they'll
scarce believe
their eyes!
It's called a Magic
Lantern Show, the latest thing of all,
Far better than the shadow pictures Dad makes on the wall . . .

But now shopping's over — time to call it a day,
Let's hope they've remembered the mistletoe spray!

— Kathleen O'Farrell.

"Chris is fourteen." Bryce shrugged. "At least they'll always remember this Christmas."

But I had wanted them to have a magical, fairy tale Christmas, unforgettable because it had been so wonderful, not because it had, as Chris put it, stunk.

That night, as I tried to go to sleep despite the penetrating cold, I was determined to regain the Christmas I had imagined for us all, or at least part of it.

Another six inches of snow fell overnight, dashing any hopes that the roads would be clear that day. It was Christmas Eve, which meant no tree or going to the midnight carol service. Chris and Alisa both had faces that bordered on the positively tragic.

"It's warmed up a bit," I said determinedly. "Why don't we try clearing the rink again?"

"What for?" Chris gave me a disgusted look. "It'll just snow again."

"It's something to do," I said lightly. "And if we all help, we could get it done in time for a game before dark."

Grudgingly, Chris went to get his snow gear on.

A few minutes later we were all outside in the dazzling sunshine. The sun bounced off the snow, making everything glitter. Wrapped up warmly, and heated through with the physical exercise of clearing the snow from the lake, I don't think any of us felt the cold.

We all worked hard, determined to get the rink cleared. Even Alisa hefted quite a few shovelfuls, her little face pink with exertion . . . and cold.

I GAZED around me in amazement, one hand resting on my shovel. If possible, Silver Lake was even more beautiful in winter than in summer. The trees were encased in ice, lending a sense of wonder to the world.

Cottages whose porches were usually heaped with bikes, deckchairs, fishing rods and walking boots could now barely be seen beneath the huge, pristine drifts of snow.

The sky was a brilliant blue, and everything else was stark, startling white. The purity of colour took my breath away.

"We're done!" Chris shouted.

I turned and saw that he had cleared the last few feet of snow and jubilantly tossed his shovel in a snow bank. We had a rink, definitely smaller than the first attempt, but good enough to play on.

"Let's play!" Chris cried, and we all ran to get our skates.

Generously, Chris and Bryce gave Alisa and me the hockey sticks and they took the brooms, but they still clobbered us, as I had fully expected.

As night began to fall, a sunset trail blazing across the snow, we trooped inside for hot chocolate.

Later, as I was making dinner, Chris and Alisa called me into the living-room.

"Come and see, Mummy!" Alisa called excitedly. "We have something to show you."

"It's not much," Chris mumbled, looking both embarrassed and proud at the same time.

Tears trembled on my lashes and I blinked them back. Chris and Alisa had made a Christmas tree out of some cut pine boughs from outside, stuck in a bucket. They had decorated the boughs with some of the ornaments and tinsel I had brought, and Chris had even fashioned a foil star for the top.

He was right, it wasn't much, and yet it was everything. It showed me that they were glad to be here, that they had entered into the spirit of things, and that together we could still have the most wonderful Christmas ever.

"I love it," I said, my voice wavering slightly. "It's wonderful."

✳ ✳ ✳ ✳

From then on, we never looked back. The lack of running water, the overwhelming cold and snow . . . none of it could take away from what was truly becoming a magical Christmas.

In fact, I realised, all those things which had seemed like hardships actually added to it, making this Christmas even more special.

Since we couldn't get to the Christmas service at the nearby church, Bryce had the brilliant idea of holding our own.

Alisa had a wonderful time decorating her homemade service sheets, and Bryce played some carols on his guitar. Chris even joined in the singing, which was a definite first, and afterwards Bryce read the Bible story while we listened quietly, not a sound to be heard in the world except for the hiss and crackle of the fire.

I could almost imagine what it must have been like back then, two thousand years ago, on a night as peaceful and still as this one.

That night, Chris and Alisa went to bed as giddy as tiny children for the next morning, and the opening of their presents. Chris and I tiptoed around our makeshift Christmas tree, putting out their gifts, as excited as children ourselves.

That night the cold didn't seem so terrible as I lay in Bryce's arms.

"You know what?" he whispered. "This crazy idea of yours wasn't so bad after all."

I smiled in the darkness.

"It could have been," I allowed, "except for all of you. It took all of us to make this Christmas work."

Actually, I thought, this Christmas didn't just work . . . it was wonderful. I wouldn't have exchanged it for the warmest house, the biggest tree, or all the luxuries in the world.

No, I thought with a sleepy smile, we preferred to be just like pioneers.

I snuggled closer to Bryce and closed my eyes, at peace with the world. ■

Time For A Change

by Margaret Langley.

EMILY GIBSON yawned and stretched, then rolled over to check the time on her bedside alarm clock. Half past ten, which was late for her, but the party they'd had last night hadn't finished until three.

Thank goodness her mum had stayed the night. She would have got the children up and sorted out breakfast by now. Strange how quiet it was, though. Usually the children were a lot noisier than this.

Emily thought she had better get up and see what was going on. She slid out of bed without waking her husband and put her feet into the new fur-lined slippers that had been one of her Christmas presents.

Heavens, she thought, I must be getting old — fur-lined slippers as a present! Casting her mind back, she thought longingly of the silk underwear and pieces of jewellery that Steve used to buy her before the children were born.

Had she changed that much? Steve obviously thought so. But she was only thirty years old — was she really ready for fur-lined slippers for Christmas? He must be trying to tell her something.

It was New Year's Day today. Given the slippers, it was time she made some dramatic changes in her life! First thing on the list was obviously a new hairstyle.

And she'd have to stop talking about potty training, or Jess and Sam's latest funny sayings. She'd keep those stories for Grandma instead — she'd appreciate them.

As well as the new hairstyle, she'd also treat herself to some new perfume — something expensive and unusual, not the bottle of

Illustration by Gerard Fay.

whatever-had-been-on-special-offer Steve bought her for Christmas last year!

It may have been New Year's Day, but Emily couldn't help but feel thoroughly disgruntled.

A NEW dress would help. At least it would get her out of the boring jeans and sweaters she wore every day. She'd choose a real colour, too, not a dark sensible one that didn't show the dirty marks when you picked up small kids with muddy feet, either.

Scarlet, that was it — warm red wool, very soft. Or should she go for one of those shimmery materials? Where would she buy it? Obviously something more upmarket than her usual shops on the high street was required.

Perhaps she should go the whole hog and have a day out in London. No wonder Tony Blair was always going to Italy. Cherie must love having access to Pisa, Genoa and Milan.

Emily wished she lived in Italy, with all those lovely little boutiques to choose from, and lots of individual styles so you didn't turn up wearing exactly the same outfit as the girl at the next table in the restaurant.

But, she sighed, what chance was there of turning up at a restaurant? By the time you'd paid for the babysitter there was no money left to eat out.

Oh, we'll find it somewhere, she thought as, newly showered, she squirted on the scented body lotion her mother had bought her. At least she wouldn't smell of baby lotion or shampoo.

And what about her legs? She'd given them a hasty going over with the razor in the shower, but a regular appointment with a beauty therapist to have them waxed would make them feel much better. And it would make her feel better, too, she thought — being the one who was being pampered and looked after for a change.

She looked at herself critically in the mirror as she dried her hair, unable to decide whether to have highlights or change the colour completely.

I am quite small really, she thought. It would be nice to get out of the flatties I've been wearing for the last four years and into some smart shoes again. There was a beautiful pair of evening sandals she'd seen in a magazine that would really show off her legs — and they were one of her best features.

GOING downstairs, she found her mother up to her elbows in soapy water.

"I thought I might as well give you a hand with the clearing up, Emily," she said.

The children were playing quietly and contentedly, the way they always did when Mum was in charge. Sam was building his junior Lego at the kitchen table and little Jessica was on the floor, taking things out of a box. Emily wished she could perform whatever magic it was that her mother possessed.

Deciding that there was no time like the present, Emily spoke to her mum about looking after the children for a day while she went into the city to check out the sales.

She even managed to talk her mum into it before a bleary-eyed Steve came down the stairs in search of a cup of tea and the aspirins.

* * * *

Her day out three days later was a complete success. She had made an appointment with the hairdresser beforehand and her hair was now highlighted and cut in a fashionable style.

She hadn't found the scarlet dress she had dreamed of but had settled for a very dark red which looked really good with her new hair colour. She had also bought some very attractive black high-heeled shoes to wear with it and squandered the last of her money on a bottle of the latest Chanel fragrance.

The train brought her home just as her mum was getting ready to leave.

"I've put the chicken in the oven and peeled the veg," Mum said before she hurried off.

THE children were already eating their meal, so when they finished Emily bathed them and got them ready for bed. Then she set the table and put candles on it. She and Steve could have a romantic dinner together. She couldn't remember the last time they'd done that.

There was only enough time to change into her finery, spray on the new perfume and check her reflection in the mirror before she heard Steve's key in the door.

He was hanging his coat in the hall cupboard as, deliberately making an entrance, she came slowly downstairs.

"Hello, love," he said. "Is dinner ready? I've to go straight back to work to show a couple round number fourteen."

She didn't bother to light the candles, just served up the meal, which Steve ate at top speed.

"Kids in bed?" he asked. "I'll just take a quick look at them before I dash off." Then he ran upstairs, leaving Emily feeling as deflated as a burst balloon.

"All quiet," he said, putting his coat on again, and kissing her perfunctorily before disappearing out the door.

Left alone, Emily trailed upstairs disconsolately and hung the new dress in its plastic cover in the wardrobe. She put her new shoes back in their box and changed into her jeans and sweater.

Defiantly, she squirted on a cloud of her new perfume and went downstairs to spend another evening with the crossword and the TV. She seemed to be spending a lot of evenings on her own just now. She knew the children were small and that this stage of their lives would pass quickly, but it was so depressing to feel that she was trapped in this house — to feel that they never went anywhere any more as a couple. A night out for just the two of them would be so lovely . . .

Was Steve really working all these extra shifts? Were the fur-lined slippers a sign that he had lost interest and was seeing someone else? She tried to push the jealous suspicions out of her mind and concentrated on her crossword.

TWO days later, as she was pulling the washing out of the laundry basket, she found something hidden at the bottom. It was a parcel, wrapped in brown paper.

"What on earth . . ?" she wondered aloud.

Puzzled, she opened it and fingered the lace on the beautiful underwear it contained. Those suspicious thoughts that had been preying on her mind came flooding back. Who was this for? Had she been right about Steve?

Then she spotted the envelope. With reluctant fingers she opened it and, through her tears, read the card.

I did notice, it said, *and you can wear these with your new dress when we dine out on Saturday night.* ■

Printed and Published in Great Britain by D.C. Thomson & Co., Ltd., Dundee, Glasgow and London.

ISBN 0 85116 854 X
EAN 9 780851 168548

J. CAMPBELL KERR.